"Not so high-and-mighty today, are you, princess?"

His green eyes glittered with a fury she had seen once before, on the day she'd left him. And this was no homecoming. Not the kind she'd imagined all these years. This was vengeance. "You destroyed me, Amalia. I promised you that if you ever gave me the opportunity, I would return the favor. And here you are."

"Joaquin." She tried again, though it seemed that every time she spoke his name, his grip on her tightened. Just enough to remind her. Of how commanding he was. How...bossy. How he had set the terms of their trysts and then executed them and she had melted, and burned, and happily done as he pleased.

Because it was what she pleased, too.

He tipped her chin up, his eyes a green fire. And yet even if he hated her now, her body couldn't tell the difference. This fire was still a fire, and she burned for him the way she always had.

The Lost Princess Scandal

Swapped at birth...but now the secret is out!

Delaney Clark has grown up on a farm in the Midwest. The idea she has royal blood is absurd to her...until Cayetano Arcieri tells her the shocking truth. She is the long-lost princess of Ile d'Montagne, and if she accepts his hand in marriage, he can offer her a crown and a passion more incendiary than anything she's ever imagined. But will that be enough for Delaney to accept?

Find out in *Crowning His Lost Princess*!

When Princess Amalia of Ile d'Montagne discovers she's not a princess at all, her priority is finding a place where she can hide away and plan a new future. She does *not* expect to be sharing that place with the unforgettable Spaniard from her past, Joaquin Vargas...or for their illicit chemistry to still burn as brightly as it ever did. But is it hot enough to scorch through the barriers keeping them apart?

Find out in *Reclaiming His Ruined Princess*!

Both available now!

Caitlin Crews

RECLAIMING HIS RUINED PRINCESS

ISBN-13: 978-1-335-56967-7

Reclaiming His Ruined Princess

Harlequin Enterprises ULC
22 Adelaide St. West, 41st Floor
Toronto, Ontario M5H 4E3, Canada
www.Harlequin.com

Printed in U.S.A.

USA TODAY bestselling, RITA® Award–nominated and critically acclaimed author **Caitlin Crews** has written more than one hundred books and counting. She has a master's and PhD in English literature, thinks everyone should read more category romance and is always available to discuss her beloved alpha heroes. Just ask. She lives in the Pacific Northwest with her comic book artist husband, is always planning her next trip and will never, ever, read all the books in her to-be-read pile. Thank goodness.

Books by Caitlin Crews

Harlequin Presents

Chosen for His Desert Throne
The Sicilian's Forgotten Wife
The Bride He Stole for Christmas

Pregnant Princesses

The Scandal That Made Her His Queen

Rich, Ruthless & Greek

The Secret That Can't Be Hidden
Her Deal with the Greek Devil

The Lost Princess Scandal

Crowning His Lost Princess

Visit the Author Profile page
at Harlequin.com for more titles.

To Jackie, the patron saint of a certain kind of scene. Consider this a homage.

CHAPTER ONE

Amalia Montaigne only realized how much she loved her life when it was taken from her.

She supposed there was a lesson in that, little as she enjoyed learning it. She had been raised as the Crown Princess of Ile d'Montagne, a tiny island country in the Mediterranean, with her every move pored over and scrutinized by friend, foe, and paparazzo alike as she learned how to walk in the footsteps of her formidable mother, Queen Esme.

Her main concern throughout her life so far had been the attempt to carve out a space in that fishbowl existence to be *her.* Not the Princess, bound by duty and convention. Not the public figure, owned by anyone and everyone who looked at her. A woman with a real life of her own, however hidden away from view.

But *real life* wasn't easy to come by for

a woman in her position. Her single experience with it had ended badly. And as far as she could tell, her mother had abdicated her own real life, such as it was, in service to the crown long ago. All Esme spoke of was her throne, her legacy—not as a mother, but as a queen. If she had private thoughts about anything else, she usually kept them to herself.

Amalia had been determined that *she* would not do the same. *She* would live up to the expectations placed upon her *as well* as create a place, somewhere in the swirl of duty and honor and obligation, where she could be entirely herself.

She hadn't been succeeding in that objective, but now it no longer mattered. The truth had come out, shocking the world and turning her life—real or otherwise—inside out. Princess Amalia of Ile d'Montagne had been switched at birth. Or, rather, three days after her birth, to be precise—with the daughter of a farmer from Kansas. And the girl who had been raised on that farm, the true blue-blooded heir to the throne Amalia had been training to take over her whole life, had gone and married the head of the rebel faction that had been tormenting the Ile d'Montagne royal family for centuries.

Meaning that not only was Amalia not the

Crown Princess, the future of her country and her mother's successor, but the true Princess had returned to claim what was hers with the Montaigne family's sworn enemy—a neat little bloodless, slow-moving coup that would change the little island country forever. It already had.

Not that it mattered to the actual, real life Amalia who was still a headline at the moment. She assumed she wouldn't remain one for long. The fascination with her would pass quickly, she had no doubt, and all that attention would shine on someone else, instead. Probably actual princesses, including the one she had been unwittingly masquerading as all this time. Amalia's name would be trotted out every decade or so to kick up the scandal anew and sell papers, that was all. Especially once Delaney Clark, the true heir, became Queen. And the more obscure Amalia became in the meantime, the more the greedy tabloid consumers would love it.

Can you believe *that* she *was almost a queen?* they would tut on their morning commutes, or standing in their checkout lines.

The upshot of all this was, for the first time in her life, Amalia could have been anyone at all.

What she felt most keenly, however, was

that she was a newly twenty-five-year-old woman who had no idea what to do now that her destiny wasn't mapped out before her, step by step, until death. Now she had nothing to do, for the rest of her life, but be *herself.*

Whoever *that* was.

"Are you ready?"

Amalia smiled at the aide who stood with her in the small hall off the entryway to the palace that the royals used for more private entrances and exits. Paparazzi were expressly forbidden. Both Amalia and the impassive woman beside her were pretending. The aide that it was perfectly normal that the once future Queen was slipping away so ignominiously tonight, with no fanfare and no farewell committee. And Amalia that she was serene about her change in circumstances.

But then, she had no choice but to act serene. It was that or go kicking and screaming, and what would that get her except pity and scorn? Amalia thought she could handle almost anything but pity. She felt lucky, truly, that her mother hadn't offered her any—as she rather thought it might have killed her.

And she was immune to scorn. A life in the gimlet crosshairs of the public eye had made certain of that. But who knew—maybe a heaping of scorn as a private citizen would do her in too.

Best to put a good face on it, she'd decided.

Amalia was doing her best not to think about it all too closely while she was still here. Still in the palace where she'd been raised. The palace she considered her home. Instead, she concentrated on waiting gracefully, because she knew her behavior in these final moments would be dissected and retold, no matter how professional the aide was acting while still in her presence. She folded her hands before her and pressed her tongue to the roof of her mouth to keep her jaw from tightening around her polite smile. She'd used to think of such tricks, used while forever being in public and watched so closely, as making her mother proud.

Though she had to remind herself—yet again—that Queen Esme of Ile d'Montagne was not her mother. No matter the twenty-five years they'd spent together. It was all washed away as if it had never been. A few blood tests were all it had taken to erase their relationship.

It was stunning, really. Breathtaking. Impossible to fully comprehend.

Because at first, the Queen had been defiant. *Shall the throne of Ile d'Montagne be toppled by these grubby upstarts?* Esme had thundered. *Not on my watch.*

If it's a scam, it's masterfully done, Amalia had hedged. *Truly.*

She could remember that moment so clearly. She and the Queen had been taking their morning meal together, as was their long-held custom. They sat together in the Queen's private salon so that Esme could rage about her enemies—almost always the rebels in the mountains, but sometimes the insufficiently reverent European press—and lecture Amalia on topics ranging from Esme's strategy for finding suitable marital prospects for her only child to comprehensive critiques of Amalia's public appearances.

Amalia had learned long ago when to treat these lectures as conversations and when it was better to sit there quietly and listen to Her Majesty deliver a monologue.

'Masterful' is not a word I would apply to the likes of Cayetano Arcieri and his obsessive fever dreams of someday taking my throne, Esme had sniffed that day.

But Cayetano, rebel warlord and thorn in the side of the royal family, had played his hand well. He had married his not-quite-a-farm-girl in secret in his stronghold in the hills. Only once the true Princess had been bound to him forever had he given that fateful interview to a friendly British paper that had been hanging on his every word since university. And in that one, specifically devastating interview, he had dropped—almost as an afterthought—the news that the woman he'd married was, believe it or not, the longlost daughter of none other than Esme herself.

Esme, who had suffered the sort of pregnancy complications that had necessitated she fly to America, to the only hospital in the world that specialized in that exact syndrome, the better to protect her heir. And because of this, was there at the same time as the other mother—*my real mother,* as Amalia tried to remember to think of her. The nurse who was suspected of having made the mistake and given the real Princess to the wrong mother couldn't defend herself, having died years ago.

Two babies switched in a hospital, Cayetano had said in that interview, with the quiet charm that was a hallmark of his media appearances. In person, Amalia had always found him more off-putting. Much colder and more…warlord-like, which made sense. *Who could imagine such a thing?*

And since Cayetano had spent the better part of his life building up his media relationships in all the right places, making himself the protagonist in the story of Ile d'Montagne instead of the villain Amalia had always believed him to be, his accusation caught fire.

I can't imagine what he's playing at, Esme had seethed the morning after that appearance, slapping her hand on the stack of newspapers before her. *An accusation like this is so easily disproven. What a fool.*

That night Amalia had stood in her rooms, finally alone after a long day forever surrounded by courtiers and aides, fussy ministers and the occasional subject. And she'd thought it sounded lovely to grow up on a farm in a place like Kansas, which she knew chiefly from *The Wizard of Oz*—a film she'd watched at least a hundred times on her own. She'd gazed out of her window, looking out over the sparkle of Ile d'Montagne's royal city with its blue roofs and white buildings by day and gleaming lights by night. And she'd thought, *Wouldn't that be funny, if Mother was the wicked witch after all?*

But she hadn't really thought it could be true. How could she be someone else when there had been battalions of tutors and aides and ministers to make sure she was exactly who she was supposed to be? Always and forever?

Then had come the blood tests—then several repeats of the same blood tests. There had been endless speculation in the press. Amalia had tracked the inconceivable truth through Esme's growing distance. The Queen became too busy in her mornings to break her fast with Amalia. And then, after a while, Amalia had been sent out on a deeply uncomfortable meeting with Delaney Clark, Kansas farm girl turned future queen, to show that the crown accepted reality. And did so with grace and self-deprecating humor, Amalia's specialty.

Amalia had seen Esme alone only once more. The Queen had called her into her formal rooms, where heads of state came to pay their respects and underlings were dressed down for all manner of slights and missteps. Amalia was treated as a member of the latter group and made to stand some distance away. As if they had never been anything to each other.

And the woman she still thought of as her mother had not made the slightest attempt to reach out to her or comfort her in any way. Then again, Esme had not been big on reaching out or offering comfort the past twenty-five years, either. That was not one of her strengths.

You will always be cared for, Esme had told her, stiffly. Maybe that was her version of comfort. *You need have no worries in this life, Amalia. I will guarantee you that. I am deeply cognizant that nothing that has occurred is any way your fault.*

That would be a long game indeed, Amalia had said quietly, her gaze respectfully lowered in the presence of the sovereign, no matter the churn of emotions within her. *Especially if I started said game at three days old.*

Once, Esme would have pounced on a comment like that. That day, when Amalia snuck a look, the Queen's eyes had been cool and she had only smiled that tight smile she mainly used to stop courtiers at ten paces.

It wasn't that Amalia had expected a hug. Esme was not tactile, as she liked to tell dignitaries from effusive countries when they attempted to get too close. Amalia knew better than to hope that might change…but she did anyway.

Nonetheless, Esme had told her frostily, clearly not in any kind of *hugging* mood, *it has been decided that it would be best if you took a step back.*

Of course, Amalia had said, because what

else could she say? *I serve at your pleasure. Or do not.*

It was the last time she saw her mother. Because Her Majesty the Queen was always too busy for anyone not deemed essential. And wasn't that a bit of a shock? To discover that after all these years, all she'd given—and more, had given up—she could be hustled away and thrust out of sight so easily?

It wasn't only Esme. When Amalia was feeling charitable, she rather thought that the Queen didn't know quite what to do. What was there to say or do, after all? The reality of those blood tests had to have shaken the proud Queen to the core. Because Esme hadn't noticed that her baby had been replaced. She hadn't noticed that she was raising an imposter. Surely that said more about her than the daughter she was now distancing herself from.

The newspapers certainly thought so.

Amalia went from having two extra mobiles manned entirely by staff—so they could handle the endless influx of calls—to barely needing her own, private mobile at all. Since no one called her. Because no one knew who *she* was. They only knew she wasn't the Princess.

She was used to having parades of men

circling around her, jockeying for position because one of them would be chosen—eventually—by the Queen to become the Crown Princess's husband. And would therefore one day be King. Amalia had always found these men irritating, so it was a surprise to discover that she noticed their absence so keenly. Even though Esme had finally narrowed it down to two acceptable suitors in the past year. And while Amalia had really never cared much for those two, both of vague royal blood in one way or another, they had been so solicitous. So generous and thoughtful.

Yet neither one of them had bothered to reach out once the news broke.

It was clarifying.

And perhaps this was a gift, she tried to tell herself as she waited, stuck in limbo until the Queen decided it was time for her to exit quietly. One she would look back on someday with gratitude. Because she had always wondered how much she truly mattered to anyone, taken apart from her bloodline. And now she knew.

Like it or not, she knew.

"Just a few more moments," the aide beside her said now, her fingers on the earpiece she wore. "Then you can be on your way at last."

As if Amalia was setting off on a pleasant

holiday. And not being shuffled out the back door in disgrace. That it was none of her own making was neither here nor there.

The palace had planned her exit carefully. The Queen was welcoming Cayetano Arcieri and the new Crown Princess of Ile d'Montagne—his wife, Delaney—with a grand reception now that the two of them had returned to the island after an extended honeymoon. It was the first time an Arcieri had set foot in the ancient palace since the famous feud between his people and Esme's had begun.

No one would pay the slightest attention to Amalia as she faded off into the night. Which was precisely how everyone wanted it.

Amalia was to simply…disappear.

Her Majesty has seen fit to provide you with a most generous situation, her mother's most fearsome minister had told her. He was the one who did the talking, though he'd come into the meeting with a phalanx of palace attorneys to back him up. As if, Amalia had thought, she had been attempting blackmail instead of just…reeling. *The expectation is that you will handle these unforeseen developments with grace.*

My mistake, Amalia had murmured. *I thought the Queen was taking care of me because I have trained my whole life to be a person that I am not. I didn't realize it was a bribe for future good behavior.*

The minister had gazed at her with a certain amount of steely forbearance. *Her Majesty is cognizant of the fact that you might have a number of feelings concerning recent events, Amalia. So do we all.*

Amalia had spent the previous few weeks overseeing the packing up of her things. Which had involved a great deal of thinking about what was actually hers. Because so much of what she considered her own was in fact her mother's. Or the palace's. Or, more properly, belonged to the people of Ile d'Montagne.

People who were not hers.

She tried, very hard, to be fair.

But she also had to bear in mind that she was not moving house, as regular people did all the time, or so she was informed. She was taking what was reasonably hers—and what the Queen, through surrogates, wished to bestow upon her—and shipping it off to a storage facility outside Paris. Because *outside Paris* seemed as good a center of operation as any, because wasn't that what people needed? A home base of some kind? Having never thought beyond Ile d'Montagne, she hardly knew how she was expected to figure out where she ought to live.

Much less how.

Amalia felt certain that she could learn how to do all those things that were considered normal. Like pay bills. Or...have bills in the first place. And a place for those bills to find her. One thing she had gathered from watching television over the years was that most people were preoccupied with bills. She imagined that she would be too, then.

But she was going to have to figure that out on her own. It was that or have someone teach her, and how could she tell if such a person would have her best interests at heart? She was a suddenly ex-princess with zero street smarts. No one had to tell her that she was ripe for the picking. She imagined there would be all sorts of people lining up to take advantage of her.

Anyway, she found herself less than sympathetic to the notion that the palace staff might have found any of this as difficult as she did.

If I'm understanding you correctly, she'd said dryly, *the concern is that I will fling myself into the sort of antics that I was always expressly forbidden. And in so doing, bring shame upon the House of Montaigne.*

The only concern of the Queen, as I think we both know.

That you are not the blood relation of Her Majesty may be well known, the minister had replied. *But I think you know that doesn't matter. You will be scrutinized for the rest of your life. You will be compared to the new Crown Princess. And then, one day, to the new Queen. That may not be fair, but it is reality. There is no virtue in pretending otherwise.*

Wonderful, Amalia had said, with her practiced smile. *At least all these years of training won't be entirely useless. I'll be able to act as appropriately as ever, forever in service to this country which, it turns out, has nothing to do with me at all.*

The minister had surprised her then. He had looked at her with what she very much thought was genuine compassion.

You have always impressed us all with your grace and character, he said quietly, knocking her smile off her face. *I have every reason to believe that no matter what you do, you'll never change such an essential part of who you are. If I were you, my lady, I would look at this not as a punishment at all. But as freedom.*

That was the word that echoed inside of Amalia tonight. *Freedom.*

Whatever that was.

She nodded at the aide beside her when she was finally given the go-ahead. She smiled the way she always had, serene and easy— a smile she'd practiced for years in the mirror. Then she walked out of the palace and climbed into the waiting car that would sneak her away from everything she knew, down to the docks where a boat waited to take her off of this island and far from Ile d'Montagne. Likely forever.

Amalia couldn't think of a single reason she would ever return. Not when she could only be a sad shadow lurking about the island she had loved, a reminder of so many years of unwitting deception.

But that was all right, she told herself stoutly as she boarded the small yacht that waited for her, far from the royal docks and staffed with the most trustworthy of the Queen's men. Because she was setting sail for *freedom.*

Not that she'd had a great lot of experience with the concept. *Freedom,* her tutors had told her sternly when she was growing up and needed to be more like a queen and less

like the bored child she was, *is for others, far
less privileged. It is not for you.*

And aside from one golden summer, that
had been true.

Amalia didn't stand out on the yacht's
deck. She didn't want to be seen—it would
disappoint the Queen and she still cared about
that. More than she should. And besides, she
didn't want to look back at the island. At the
life that had never been hers.

At everything she was losing tonight.

She curled herself up in her stateroom and
settled in for the night. Because there, in private, she could indulge herself the way she'd
tried so hard not to all these years.

Oh, how she'd tried—and failed.

But tonight there was no one to scold her.
No one to remind her of her duty—because
she had no more duties. She had the Queen's
request to avoid scandals that might reflect
badly on Ile d'Montagne, though she was no
longer required to honor the Queen's request.
She wasn't the Queen's subject. Oh, and she
had freedom, whatever that was.

What was that song that suggested it was
nothing more than nothing left to lose?

So—for once without the usual guilt—
Amalia thought about that summer.

And better yet, him.

Joaquin Vargas.

Even his name made her shiver, across space and time.

She had been twenty and sheltered. Guarded her whole life.

The Crown Princess was always supervised. Never left to her own devices, for fear that any decisions she might make on her own would lead to embarrassment for the palace.

Far too many European royals work out their adolescent drama on the front pages of the tabloids, the palace media manager had told her severely when she was still a girl. *Her Majesty the Queen does not intend for Ile d'Montagne to join these ranks. Do you understand, Your Highness?*

Amalia had understood. How could she not? The contours of the glass bowl she lived in had always been clear to her. And it only took a few unflattering turns on a tabloid cover to understand that there was very little benefit to smashing her face up against that glass. It could leave unsightly marks. It might even cause a commotion. But what it didn't do, ever, was change her circumstances.

The summer of her twentieth year, the rebel faction in the mountains had been louder than usual. And the warlord, Cayetano, was entirely too good at whipping up international sympathy for his cause. It had driven her mother mad.

Maybe that was why it was agreed that the Crown Princess could have a holiday, instead of following her mother around from engagement to engagement as usual.

As long as I do not hear of any yachting about the Côte d'Azur, the Queen had said gravely. *Like some common Hollywood tart.*

And looking back now, Amalia couldn't remember how she'd found Cap Morat. Once thought to have been connected to the Spanish mainland, the island had been a fortress for many ages, then had fallen into disrepair. It had been bought at some point before that summer and transformed into a luxurious hotel experience boasting the height of privacy there in the Balearic Sea.

The palace had rented the whole of the island for the summer, so that her guards could keep themselves to the perimeter—meaning mostly on boats and the odd beach—and Amalia could wander about and pretend she was normal.

As the only guest on the island, she'd made friends with the staff immediately.

But it had been the owner who had captivated her.

Joaquin Vargas. She couldn't remember,

now, what she had known about him at the time and what she had learned in the five years since. That he was self-made. That he had come from nothing and only by sheer force of will had he made himself into a myth. A legend. Capable of transforming a rock in the sea and a crumbling old fortress into an opulent retreat for the wealthiest and most famous—and that was but one of the tricks he'd used to cement his position as the darling of the financial world.

Though what she remembered chiefly about him from that very first meeting was the green of his eyes, gleaming with intent and too much fire from a face that seemed cut from stone. And polished to shine.

It was not too sentimental to admit that she had fallen at first sight. It was a fact. One moment she had been who she always was, eating a breakfast out on the patio overlooking the sea. She had been enjoying the touch of the breeze against her face. The song of birds in the trees. She had been trying her best to fully inhabit this freedom she knew would not come again. Amalia had been thinking about her mother's insistence in choosing a husband for her only daughter. And how little interest she had in any of the candidates her mother favored.

Same old, same old.

Then she looked up and Joaquin was there. And nothing that summer was ever the same.

She was never the same.

She shivered again, now, in her comfortable berth in the boat that took her across the water, heading for that same rock set down in the sea. She drew her soft cashmere wrap tighter around her and tried to take the sort of deep, cleansing breaths that one of the personal trainers she'd worked with over the years always claimed held near-magical properties.

Amalia could admit, privately, here in the privacy of her own head, that there was a part of her that wished that she was running to Joaquin after all this time.

When she knew that if she tried such a thing, he would likely set her on fire as soon as look at her.

That was the choice she'd made. The only choice she could have made, she told herself now as she had then, but that didn't make it any less harsh. Because summer had ended. There had been no possibility Queen Esme would ever accept a self-made Spanish businessman as an appropriate mate for her only heir. No possible way that she would even entertain the conversation.

Amalia had gotten one perfect summer. And that was more than she had ever dared hope she would get. But she and Joaquin had loved each other so well, so deeply, and with such earth-shattering intensity that she had known there was no way he would ever accept the idea that she would *choose* to leave him.

Because she wouldn't—if she had been anyone else. If she had been anything but a crown princess, heiress to a throne and subject to her mother's decrees in all things. She had ended it abruptly, and unkindly. And had fled back to her duties, her responsibilities, her plotted-out life and suitors she hadn't wanted even before she'd met a man like Joaquin.

She sighed as she closed her eyes and remembered. And she could pretend, as she lay in her bunk, that she was returning to those syrupy gold, endlessly sweet days five years ago. She'd pretended exactly that on more occasions than she could count. Joaquin was her secret and she'd kept him tucked away inside her like a precious jewel too dear to expose to the light.

When instead, the truth was that she had rented herself a little villa on the island under a false name, because that might keep the tabloids at bay. And she expected no syrupy sweetness, because she did not expect that she would run into the island's owner at all. Not after the way she'd left him five years ago. This time she merely intended to hide away from the other guests and the whole of the world, until she felt strong enough to face what was happening to her. And perhaps, somewhere in there, able to come up with some kind of plan for the future.

Because hers was no longer plotted out for her, step by step, until her death. Maybe, at some point, she would find such a freedom exhilarating. Until then, she intended to stare at the sea, hide herself away from the intrusion of press and idle speculation, and heal in the only place she'd ever let herself imagine…*what if?*

She might even consider seeking out her real mother at some point, she supposed. A woman with a farm in Kansas, which was as fanciful a location as another planet to Amalia. But first, she supposed, she needed to let go of the mother she'd had in Queen Esme all these years. Distant, difficult. Often demanding. Always formidable.

But still, her mother for a quarter of a century. And Amalia loved her, for all the good it had done her. She still felt too brittle and taken aback to process any of that, but she knew it was coming. Along with a healthy dollop of grief, she imagined.

Because it was one thing to complain about your life. And another thing to have it snatched away from you with no possibility of ever getting it back. At some point, she expected she would need to mourn what was lost.

But not tonight.

Tonight, she drifted off into sleep and only woke when the boat docked at Cap Morat.

She made herself presentable and then climbed up onto the deck, sighing a bit as the island gleamed there before her, golden and glorious, just as she remembered it. The old fortress rose imposingly, burnished to shine. It was a small island, easily walkable, and she already itched to wander its paths and sit on its rocky cliffs to look out to the endless, beckoning sea. Surely she would find herself here. Surely she would encounter the woman she was meant to be as she left the Princess behind.

A shiver of foreboding worked its way down her neck. Amalia told herself it was the breeze.

It seemed particularly quiet, she thought as she stepped off the boat. She smiled vaguely around her, looking for the hotel staff that she remembered being effortlessly ubiquitous when she'd been here before. Perhaps it was different when there were other guests about.

She walked along the stone path that led from the docks straight toward the grand front entrance of the hotel. Each step was like walking through her memories. She longed to kick off her shoes and let the warm stones kiss her bare feet. She couldn't wait to take down her hair from the ruthless chignon she always wore as Princess Amalia. She wanted to swim in the sea and dry herself on sun-baked stones, letting the salt stay on her skin. She wanted to bask in the sunshine, letting it tan her skin without a single thought as to how that might make her look in endless rounds of photos that her mother had always decreed ought to look timeless.

This place was timeless, so she need not be.

That was what she was thinking when she walked in the grand, open arches that served as doors, yet were always open to the elements, inviting her in. Inside, the hotel lobby was empty. She stopped then, confused. For surely there ought to be staff here, if not down at the docks. There ought to be *someone*. She turned in a circle, taking in the ornate architecture, the high ceilings. The fireplace that seemed to hover in one wall. The fountain that splashed in the center. The sense that somehow, though she stood in an ancient fortress that had been built to keep everything out, it somehow invited in the sun, the sky, the sea.

It was only when she turned the second time that she saw a shadow detach itself from the far wall.

At first she thought she was imagining it. That she was too dizzy from the sunlight that poured down from the ramparts, memory like magic, making her silly.

But he kept coming.

And her body knew him before his name fully formed in her head.

She felt that betraying flush, rolling over her, making her pink…everywhere. Between her legs, there was a kind of keening, an ache so intense it seemed to bloom and spread. It rolled to her breasts, making them feel heavy and tender. It wrapped itself around her, pulling taught.

Still he kept coming.

And she knew this dream. She'd had this dream a thousand times and always woke up, gasping for air and shattered to discover herself alone. Always alone.

She knew this dream, but today it was different.

Because as he drew closer, she drank him in, greedily. It was still him. Still the Joaquin she remembered. It was gloriously, unquestionably him. He was still breathtakingly tall. His body was a symphony of lean muscle, from mouthwateringly wide shoulders to narrow, athletic hips. He wore an obviously, exquisitely bespoke dark suit, yet still managed to look vaguely disreputable. It was the dark hair. Or his jaw, like that of a boxer. It was the way he carried himself, perhaps, as if he was ready and able to handle whatever might come his way. Whether it be bandits or wayward princesses.

She had pored over pictures of him in these last five years. She knew the possessive way his hands splayed on the back of any woman he squired about to this event or that. And could remember how it had felt when it was her. She'd wept over such things in the privacy of her bed in the palace. She'd studied his face in every picture, looking for hints of the Joaquin she'd known. How she'd loved the sculpted lines of him, the angelic cheekbones, the sensual mouth.

But what she had never seen before was the

way those green eyes of his blazed a cold fire as he approached.

In her dreams, he never looked at her like that. In her dreams, there was only ever heat. Love. Understanding.

Forgiveness.

He kept coming until he was standing before her, and even then, he did not pause. He reached out and he was touching her again, taking her chin with his fingers and holding her still.

She could feel the bluntness of his grip. The strength in him as he moved her head one way, then another, as if inspecting her. As if she was a horse he was considering purchasing.

Amalia found herself trembling as if she was exactly that much of a thoroughbred, when she knew—when the entire world knew, for that matter—that she was no such thing.

"Not so high and mighty today, are you, Princess?" came his voice. Just as she remembered it. Rough. Low and intent. She'd heard that voice in her ears as he'd danced with her in empty ballrooms here. As he'd moved above her in the bed they'd shared that summer, taking her innocence and giving her so much more in return. Lust. Longing. Love.

A whole life. "Did I not tell you what would happen if you dared return?"

"Joaquin..." she whispered.

"Allow me to remind you." His green eyes glittered with a fury she had seen once before, on the day she'd left him. And this was no homecoming. Not the kind she'd imagined all these years. This was vengeance. "You destroyed me, Amalia. I promised you that if you ever gave me the opportunity, I would return the favor. And here you are. Humbled. Cast out. Slinking back to my island, tail between your legs, as I told you that you would."

"Joaquin," she tried again, though it seemed that every time she spoke his name, his grip on her tightened. Just enough to remind her. Of how commanding he was. How...bossy. How he had set the terms of their trysts and then executed them and she had melted, and burned, and happily done as he pleased.

Because it was what she pleased, too.

She pulled in a breath and fought for calm. And she wasn't sure she managed to get there—but the fact that she was capable of trying showed her how different things were now. How different *she* was from the girl she'd been five years ago, because she'd spent that time training to become a queen.

And queens could not allow anything to rattle them.

Not even Joaquin Vargas.

Amalia found herself grateful for all those years she'd thought wasted.

Because it was the best—and only—defense she could imagine having against this man.

"I had no expectation that you would be here," she managed to say now, because a defense might protect her but it also seemed critical that he know she hadn't come here for…this. "I intended to be a guest at this hotel, nothing more. Just a regular guest. Not like last time."

"I see the years have made you a liar." He tipped her chin up, his eyes a green fire. And yet even if he hated her now, her body couldn't tell the difference. This fire was still a fire, and she burned for him the way she always had. His mouth was merciless as he brought it closer to hers and that, too, burned bright and hot inside her. "But don't worry, Amalia. I will deal with that, too."

And then he slammed his mouth to hers.

CHAPTER TWO

EVERYTHING INSIDE HIM was a roar.

Of triumph. Of need.

And that longing he had not been able to stamp out, despite five years of trying. Five years of assuring himself that there was nothing this woman had that he would ever need again, not after she'd left him the way she did.

She had eviscerated him and Joaquin Vargas never forgot a single slight.

He had made a career out of answering each and every one. All those who had laughed at his ambitions, growing up in and out of homelessness in Bilbao. Fighting for every scrap, until it occurred to him that what he was good at was the fight. Therefore, why not make the scraps bigger?

That was how he'd battled his way to his first million. Then several more millions. He'd been reveling in that accomplishment the summer Princess Amalia had wrecked him, then compounded that sin by leveling him when she'd left.

Unforgivable offenses, by his reckoning.

Joaquin had responded the only way he could. The only way he knew how. By exponentially increasing his wealth and holdings so that now he was one of the billionaires the world took such pleasure in claiming to hate.

He imagined he would hate billionaires too, were he still where he'd begun.

But in a world where there were billionaires, Joaquin had long ago decided that he might as well be one of them. Better that than be stepped on by someone else's billionaire shoe.

But all of the focus and fury that had defined his life and meteoric rise seemed to melt away from him, because he was kissing Amalia again. And she tasted the way he remembered. Like the lie he had believed for too long, that summer. Her soft, yielding lips. The little noise she made in the back of her throat.

Her taste, God help him. Innocent, when he knew better. Unutterably sweet, still.

At least this time around he was prepared.

Joaquin set her away from him, but didn't let go of her slender shoulders. More slender than he recalled, he thought, and then hated himself for entertaining even an inkling of the concern for her she certainly didn't deserve.

"I warned you not to come back here," he reminded her, his voice raw. "Or perhaps you were not paying such close attention, so focused were you on making certain I knew my place."

Her singular blue eyes were too wide, too bright. But it was her lips that caught his attention. He had always loved them swollen from his. Today was no exception.

It was harder than it should have been to focus on anything but that as his hunger for her stormed through him as if she had never betrayed him.

But he forced himself to study her closely, because he needed to remember that the woman he looked at now—elegant from head to toe, draped in cashmere with her hair swept up into something fussy—this was the real woman. This was the Princess she had chosen over him. The girl who'd captured his heart, dancing in the moonlight with her black hair all around her like a careless shadow—she was the dream. She was someone he'd made up.

And he'd paid the price for his fancy.

"You don't understand," Amalia said quietly.

And as he watched, she blinked a few times, then straightened. Her expression shifted from the hints he'd seen of her emotions to something opaque. She looked distant, yet calm, and he felt that as a kind of loss, because she was different now. She'd been so vibrant, so bright, that summer. The very hint of his disapproval had made her tear up.

Joaquin found he didn't like the evidence that she had grown while they'd been apart. For in his head, whenever he thought of her—and he did not like to admit how often he thought of her—she was still his unexpected princess. Perhaps crueler than he'd given her credit for at first, but then, she had been so young. Perhaps no longer the innocent he'd discovered here, sitting in the sun, eating fruits far less sweet than she was.

Beneath his hands he could feel the difference in her. She was bonier, perhaps. But stronger.

"What choice did I have?" she asked him now, sounding very nearly *serene*. An insult, surely, when he was nothing like serene himself. Not in her presence. That she could act otherwise was like salt against an open wound. "There was no possibility, ever, that the Crown Princess of Ile d'Montagne could have a relationship with you outside the privacy of this island. You must know this."

"Is this where you tell me that you had no say in this matter? I think we know that is another lie. We all have choices, Amalia. It is only that some of them are more pleasant than others."

He couldn't say he liked the way she smiled at him then. It was too sad, for one thing. An almost wry curve of her lips. While in her endless blue gaze, there was a certain knowledge he did not care to identify.

When, he could not help but recall, the girl he'd known would have looked at him with eyes filled with tears had he even obliquely suggested she might have lied to him. That was how open she'd been. A bright summer's day, always.

He still missed the heat of her, the endless clear blue.

And he hated her for that weakness.

"You sound like a man who has had the pleasure of his own choices for most of his life." She inclined her head slightly, far too regal for his taste. "That sounds lovely. You will have to tell me what such a life entails. Because I find myself standing at a precipice. Behind me, a life of duty and obligation but it turns out, none of it was mine. And before me…who knows?"

None of this was going the way Joaquin had planned. The kiss burned within him, still. As if she was the one who had dealt him a punishing kiss, so that his lips might bear the stamp of it. When he had meant to do that to her.

He let go of her and stepped back, glad that the grand fountain in the center of the lobby made the tumbling noise it did, for he felt certain if it did not, he would have heard his own heart. It was beating far too fast.

When Joaquin had often thought that his enemies were right and he had nothing but ice water where his veins should have been.

"You seem to be missing your staff," she said when the silence grew between them. Proving that she no longer rushed to fill a moment of quiet, the way she had five years ago. Heedless, reckless. So eager to please. He had been braced for haughtiness from the woman who had a palace to make demands on her behalf. For peremptory orders and the kind of entitlement he had always despised. Instead, she had all but wriggled like a puppy every time he'd glanced in her direction. "If you've fallen on hard times, that was definitely not mentioned when I booked. Or in any of the papers that regularly print various takes on your hagiography."

"I cleared the island," he said gruffly.

As if it was an admission.

She smiled again, but it was as distant as the first. "Not on my account, I hope. I'm perfectly capable of hiding in plain sight. It's why I booked a villa, so that all anyone looking will see is a woman in a large sun hat, minding her own business."

"I'm afraid there are no villas available," he told her smoothly, getting his feet under him again here. At last. "If you wish to stay here, there will be…alternate arrangements."

He was glad he'd let go of her. Glad that he'd put some space between them. Because he had acted on instinct the moment she'd walked into the lobby. There had been no thought. No plan. He'd simply walked to her, put his hands on her, tasted her.

He did not regret those things. But now, reason could return. He could take this moment to truly get the measure of her.

Joaquin moved away from her, over toward the rough-hewn wall so he could lean against it and observe her as he'd intended to do from the start.

She was still, bar none, the most beautiful creature he had ever beheld. He'd seen pictures of the real Princess they'd unearthed off in America somewhere. She was lovely, certainly. Yet to his mind, that Amalia shined far brighter than her dusty old mausoleum of an assumed family had always been clear. He'd seen pictures of Queen Esme, with her regal nose and aristocratic chin, which was to say, not much of one. Amalia was etched in delicate lines, each and every one of them highlighting her perfection.

He told himself he was lucky this time. Because this time, he knew that each and every hint of delicacy in her bearing was a lie.

"Alternate arrangements?" she echoed lightly, looking almost entertained. "How mysterious."

As if this was some clever little cocktail party in that palace of hers, where every moment of biting repartee was rewarded.

When the truth was, she was in his house.

And they would play by his rules.

"I was in love with you," he told her, with bite. And all the fury of the past five years. He saw her jolt at that and thought, *Good.* But it was not nearly enough. "I would have given you the sun and the moon and the stars, had you but asked. Instead, you pulled rank. And now when I think of those things I felt, the memory leaves me nothing but shame."

He watched her face closely, looking for…
But he wasn't sure what he wanted to find.
Uneasiness? Regret?

He was Joaquin Vargas. He needed none
of those things.

She gazed back at him, her expression carefully unreadable. Or almost unreadable. Her
eyes were a shade too blue. And then, because
he saw the darkness there, he looked for other
tells. She was too still, perhaps. Her hands
were in fists even though she tucked them
against her body as she folded her arms over
that wrap she wore, as if hugging it closer.

The years had taught her to hide. But he
had always been talented at finding his way
to hidden things. She stood little chance.

"I owe you an apology," she said, but her
voice was so…unruffled. Joaquin wanted to
rage. He wanted to shout. He wanted to…
mess her up, or better still, watch her as she
messed herself up. Instead, all she did was
gaze at him, as if this was nothing but a
tranquil bit of talk. Not important. Not the
least bit meaningful. "I was young and overwhelmed. I have regretted being cruel to you
every day since."

And Joaquin could not understand why this
woman got to him the way she did. Still.

It was an outrage.

He had not anticipated the *pull* of her, like some kind of magnet. It had never crossed his mind that it would be like this. Not now, on the other side of half a decade.

When he would have said he'd long since moved on. He rarely came to Cap Morat. He had so many other properties, scattered across the globe, that one little island off the coast of Spain—the country that had tried to kill him and had nearly succeeded, way back when he was a kid—hardly appealed. He'd been so busy these intervening years, acquiring things. More money. More businesses. More line items for his various portfolios.

His own fortress that could never be torn down.

Still, when her reservation had come in, flagged because she had both security concerns and was clearly using a false name, he'd figured out who she was. And he'd known instantly how he would handle it.

Even though all this time had passed. Even though, if asked, he would have said that what he remembered from that summer here was the slight she'd administered. The cruelty she'd dealt him at the end, not because it had taken him out at the knees—though it had—but because he was not a man who took insults lying down. He had built an empire on that. For years he'd promised himself that should the opportunity arise, he would happily take revenge on this woman. The same way he made certain to take his pound of flesh from anyone who dared cross him.

It was part of what made him so formidable and so justly feared.

Her apology could not change that.

No matter how she tasted.

"I'm afraid I cannot accept your apology," he told her, thrusting his hands into the pockets of his trousers. The moment he did, he felt somehow more like himself. And less like that unhinged, lust-addled creature he became around her. Only her. He lounged there against the wall and regarded her coolly. "I do not believe you mean it."

"You are mistaken," Amalia said, but in that same way. As if nothing that happened here could possibly affect her, so offensively placid was she.

"I am very rarely mistaken." He bit off the words as if they were curses. "Though when it comes to you, I will confess, I am forever imagining you to be something other than what you are."

Her brows rose slightly. Only slightly. "Why am I certain that is not meant to be flattering?"

Joaquin could not remember her being quite so dry, back then. But then, his memories were so physical. He remembered the cries she made when he thrust within her. How greedily she'd taken him. How wildly she'd come apart beneath his hands.

She'd been a princess then, but she had acted unlike any haughty noble he had ever encountered before. Maybe that was what struck him today. There was no hint of that heedless girl, reckless with wonder. There was only the Princess she'd become.

What a shame to have put in all that work and be cast out all the same, he thought.

Not with any sympathy.

"If all this is a precursor to you telling me that you will not permit me to stay at one of your properties, I understand," she told him, as if she was doing him a favor. "Though I'm not sure why you felt you needed to deliver that information with a kiss, instead of the customary email."

Neither was he, but he did not intend to share that with her.

"You can stay," Joaquin growled. "It is only that there are conditions."

Her blue eyes gleamed, as she drifted toward him, looking every inch the elegant blue blood she wasn't. Not really. That chignon, just so. The cashmere wrapped around her. The quietly elegant dress and understated heels he knew at a glance were Italian and likely made for her, personally.

"Let me guess, you intend to humble me in some way," she said, in that conversational manner she had, though her face gave nothing away.

He recognized it as a disarming tactic. Powerful women used it to charm and beguile—and he needed to remember that she had trained her whole life to be a queen. She knew all kinds of tricks. He forgot her power at his peril—and Joaquin had made a career out of knowing exactly who he was up against. It was only that he'd never wanted that to be different before.

Amalia was smiling again, that easy curve of her lips that did not match her steady blue gaze. "Your vast, incomparable male ego was bruised, and so you would take it out on me now. But you failed to consider a very important point, Joaquin."

"Unlikely."

Her smile deepened. "I have already been humbled. Everything I thought I was has been taken away from me. How do you think you can add to that?" She laughed, though it bore no resemblance to the laughter he recalled from their summer, all that sweet, spun gold. Cascading all over him like her hands on his skin or the brush of her hair over his body. "I've already been brought to my knees. Surely your little revenge fantasies are overkill to that."

"Not at all," he said softly. With intent. "My revenge fantasies are not metaphors, Princess. I want you on your actual knees."

She let out the sort of breath that might have been a gasp from a woman less in control of herself. In Amalia's case, her lips barely parted. It was hardly noticeable.

Unless, of course, a man happened to be paying as close attention as Joaquin was.

"You want me to kneel down in front of you? Right here?"

He really did. "For a start."

And as she stood there, staring back at him as if she was trying to size him up anew, Joaquin found that he was enjoying himself. The way he'd expected he would. Before that kiss he hadn't meant to indulge in.

Because whatever happened next, he'd already won. He had taken control of the situation. It was already a balm for the scars she'd left behind her.

Too much had been taken from him when he was a child. He'd vowed, as he grew, that no one would succeed in doing so again. Not when he was big enough. Not when he was strong enough. Not when he was rich enough.

And, because he was all three, he took such insults to heart. He kept the ledger, such as it was, and it felt fantastic to cross this one off his list.

Or maybe it was the way she was looking at him, as if she couldn't decide whether to flee or fling herself at him, that had him feeling that way. Either way, he liked it.

"I want to make sure that I'm understanding you," Amalia said in that same frosty way of hers.

He didn't like that she talked that way now, but he had every intention of messing that up, too. If she stayed. One thing he knew about Amalia was that she could not possibly remain frosty with him for long. Many things might have changed between them, but not that. He could feel that same chemistry the way he always did, lighting up the room they stood in. Sending off sparks that lodged themselves deep beneath his own skin.

Like it or not.

"You want there to be kneeling," she was saying, very slowly, as if encouraging him to hear what she was saying and correct himself. He did not, and her blue eyes narrowed slightly. "Because that will make you feel... better about yourself, somehow?"

"That very much depends on what you do when you're kneeling down there, Amalia," Joaquin murmured. "I feel certain you can figure something out."

"And what, pray tell, will I be getting out of this display?" she asked and laughed. Again, as if she thought this was a cocktail party. "I can understand what you might get out of it. I get the impression from all I've seen of you over the years that women do not habitually break up with you. If anything, they appear to trail about after you for years after your assignations, clinging to a pant leg if at all possible."

"I'm an excellent lover," Joaquin said. He lifted a shoulder. "But then, this you already know."

Her cheeks were pink, but she didn't shrink into herself. If anything, she stood taller. "Again, I understand the stick. What I'm not certain of here is the carrot. Is there one?"

"You tell me," he shot back, his tone almost lazy now. Because she wasn't running for the docks. She wasn't even walking away, cloaked in her rank and privilege, like the last time he'd seen her. He suspected that meant he'd won. "Everyone knows that your Queen did not boot you out the back door with nothing but the clothes on your back."

"You'd be surprised."

"Even if she did, there are any number of places you could have gone. I believe there are whole pockets of Europe that cater exclusively to deposed and discarded royalty. You came here. That sends a message, Amalia."

"I assumed your hotel would be filled with guests. And yes, I will admit it, I have a sentimental attachment to the only other period in my life when I was free to do as I pleased. It made sense to come here and bookend that." She matched his shrug with one of her own, looking cool and unruffled. It made his hands itch to dirty that up a bit. More than a bit. Because he did not care for how casually she said that when surely it was a huge admission. That she had relished her time here. That she was attached to the memory. When there was no part of any memory she could have of this island that did not involve him. "I'm sorry if you're making that more than it is."

"I'm not making it anything." Joaquin allowed himself a smile, and he doubted his was decorous. "I'm offering you a choice. You, who claim you never had a choice, can now exercise one. And so soon after leaving

Ile d'Montagne. This is the gift I'm willing to give to you. Behold my graciousness."

"A gracious gift that requires kneeling," she said after a moment, but her cheeks seemed pinker. And there was that pulse in her neck, making a nuisance of itself. Telling him things her cool tone did not. Everything in him went tight and hot. "On what looks like a rather hard floor."

"Ah, Princess. If it wasn't a hard floor, what would you learn?"

Amalia laughed again. "I didn't realize that this was a learning opportunity. How silly of me. Because it does seem to be a bit more about humiliation, to the untutored eye."

"There are few things that teach a person more than humiliation," he replied, as if he was doing her a great kindness. And perhaps he was. "But all I have asked you to do is kneel. You are the one who finds that humiliating. Suggesting that what humiliates you is you, Amalia. Not me."

"Somehow," she said after a moment, pink roses on her cheeks, but an assessing sort of look in her blue eyes, "I suspect that there's a bit more to it."

"You know me so well." Joaquin thought he saw her repress a little flinch at his sardonic tone. "It is simple enough. I will not

take your deposit. I have no interest in being
funded by that Queen of yours and her guilt
money. If you'd like to stay here, Amalia,
there was only one type of currency I will
accept." He smiled even wider then, because
here, in this moment, it felt better than he'd
imagined. And he'd imagined it would feel
spectacular. "Your body."

She stared at him for a moment, seemingly
frozen solid save for a slight widening of her
summer-blue eyes.

And he'd imagined this a thousand different ways. She would storm away in anger.
She would slink away in shame. Either way,
she would know the sting of being reduced
to nothing more than a scratched itch. She,
who had looked down her nose at him and
told him he should have known better than
to imagine the likes of him could ever mean
anything to a future queen.

Better still, he would get to witness it.

But she didn't turn on one of her elegant
heels and stalk toward the exit. Instead, her
head canted slightly to one side. Her eyes narrowed, and if he wasn't mistaken, brightened.

"From princess to prostitute in one boat
ride," she said softly. "That is quite a trajec-
tory."

His pulse picked up at that, particularly

in his sex, where it pounded like a drum. "Again, these are words you choose."

Surely she would gather herself up and walk away now. He couldn't wait.

But instead, while he gazed at her in expectation, Amalia—until recently the Crown Princess of Ile d'Montagne—closed the distance between them. She swept the wrap she wore aside, dropped it between them, and while he watched, gracefully sank to her knees.

Again, everything in him...roared.

And this was far more intense than any piddling victory.

Joaquin felt stripped down, as if she'd cut straight through him when all she'd done was obey. The way she'd always done, that summer, because it had brought all of that wildfire pleasure to them both.

"Are you trying to call my bluff, Princess?" he managed to grit out, though he was having trouble focusing on anything but the need in him. Blistering hot, all-encompassing, and, if he wasn't careful, catastrophic.

"Not at all," she replied, looking up at him, a half smile on her perfect mouth and feminine mystery in her gaze. "I currently have the freedom to do anything I want. So why not do this?"

"This is what you want?" he challenged her, from between his teeth. "To debase yourself before me?"

"It's only debasement if I feel debased," she retorted, with a flash of something he could not read in her gaze.

Maybe he was too far gone to read it.

And then, as he stood there, every muscle in his body alight with the effort to keep himself in check, she leaned forward. She put her hands on his legs, then ran her palms up his thighs, and everything in him went from a roar to a howl.

Not just need, but a kind of bone-deep possessiveness he'd told himself, in these five years, he had only ever imagined.

She ran her hands up higher and tipped her head back as she found his belt.

And all he could see was that shining blue gaze and the way she pulled her bottom lip between her teeth. She worked the belt open, unzipped him, and then pulled him free.

Her hands around him like a celebration. A homecoming.

There was a breath. A moment. It was electric.

He still thought, *She will get up now. She will walk away. She will try to turn this to her advantage—*

But the advantage was all his, even if she thought she was taking control here.

Because Amalia, his princess, tipped herself forward, still holding his gaze, and sucked him in deep.

Just the way he'd taught her.

CHAPTER THREE

LATER, AMALIA WOULD likely think this through a bit more closely. Possibly beat herself up a little, because surely when a man vowed revenge, she shouldn't throw herself on her knees and take him in her mouth as if that was the only thing she'd ever wanted to do.

But she couldn't think about that now.

Because finally, *finally,* she had Joaquin in her mouth again, and she couldn't think of a single other thing she would rather do just now than this.

Having dreamed of this at a desperate fever pitch for five long years, she did not intend to waste a single second doing anything at all but enjoying it. Enjoying him.

The taste of him, salt and man, like the sea. The thick heat of him in her mouth and the thrill of it, to see if she could stretch her mouth that wide. To test herself against his relentless length. To feel that prickle of concern that this time, she might not be able to do it—until she did.

And she knew what he liked. He had taken such care to teach her, that long-ago summer. She dropped her hands from his thighs to clasp one wrist behind her back, circling it with her other hand, well aware of the picture that made for him. And she might have worried that even that had changed, but the moment she did it his hand came to her face. He smoothed his hand over her jaw, her temple, then over her hair. Then sank his fingers into her chignon, so that he was what held her head in place.

Right where he wanted her.

And already she trembled, because she knew what would come next. Memory seemed to twine with the moment, making her burn too hot, too quick. She concentrated on the stroke of her tongue against the warm steel of him and the way he began to move, thrusting gently in and out of her mouth.

And with every thrust, he increased his pace but held her still. He set the rhythm, surrounding her with all of that heat and control, so all she could do was deliver herself into his hands and surrender to the tumult of this. The rough, raw joy.

That was the paradox of Joaquin. That was what she'd battled with all these years, longing to go and find him again despite knowing she couldn't have him. There had been the freedom of this island that summer and she had loved not having to live with security forever within sight. But the real truth was that she'd never felt more free in all her life than when this man held her in his hands and brought them both all this pleasure, more intense and beautiful than anything else she had ever known.

Even though she had known that she could never love him in return, no matter how she felt inside. No matter what she wanted.

The only thing she had ever been allowed to love was Ile d'Montagne.

Amalia felt it again now, that tidal wave of sensation, so vivid and bright that it was hard not to squirm where she knelt. She pressed her thighs together, though it was never enough—not when he was near and she knew what he could make her feel. And even though this time, she had five years of longing built up inside her, she could only make the fire dance higher and higher—she couldn't find any relief.

Then again, maybe it wasn't relief she wanted. Not when everything inside her seemed wrapped tight around that same narrow column of flame and hunger, and only Joaquin could put it out.

Or make it burn on, brighter than before.

And still he thrust in with that ruthless command, then pulled out, filling her totally and then dragging himself back, so that both of them groaned.

She lost herself in the slickness, the taste, the glory of being his again. The heat of him inside her mouth and that hard hand on the side of her face, strong fingers in her hair. This was timeless, this taking. This giving. She could feel her body respond the way it always did, trembling closer and closer to that edge only he knew the contours of—

She heard him mutter one of his favorite curses. His grip tightened.

And it was only then, only when his thrusts grew jerkier, deeper, wilder and more exhilarating, that she unclasped her hands, and moved them to his hips.

So that when he spilled himself inside her mouth, Amalia shattered apart. Even as she drank him down.

Every last drop, then took her time licking him clean.

She remembered this view of him so well. She had seen it so many times. His head thrown back and abandoned, the green of his eyes hidden behind his sooty lashes.

That mouth of his that could bring so much pleasure, flattened out in sensual starkness as he took his own.

She had been the Crown Princess of Ile d'Montagne, taught from a very young age of the power that was to be hers one day and what it meant. And yet she was not certain she had ever felt more powerful in her life than at moments like this, when she had rendered this powerful, masterful man as close to putty in her hands as he would ever be.

And now, she was nobody. Just a woman, kneeling before a man, while every nerve ending in her entire body shouted out its need and longing—because the pleasure she took in sending him spinning over the edge was only a pale echo of what it was like when he dedicated himself to the task of tearing her apart.

She remembered that all too well. Or maybe it was more accurate to say she longed for it.

And still, she felt newly dizzy with her own power here.

As nothing more than a woman who could do this to a man.

Joaquin opened his eyes and she was lost

again in all that hard green. More brilliant than ever, just now, like an emerald fire bright enough to dim the Spanish sun. His gaze held hers for a long, fiery moment. Then his lashes, wasted on a man, concealed his gaze as he reached down and handled himself.

Amalia sat back on her heels, glad she'd thought to toss her wrap to the floor. It didn't disguise the stone beneath her or alter its hardness. It was like Joaquin, really. All that stone covered in softness, like a gift.

And surely there were things they should discuss. She could think of too many, right there off the top of her head, even while her heart clattered about inside her ribs and she was still battling the urge to squirm about and *do something* with all the sensation still storming about inside her.

Maybe this time, now that she was…herself, whoever that turned out to be, she could face him with honesty and openness. And somehow wash away the things she'd said to him five years ago so he would let her go.

She didn't have to put limits on how she enjoyed him now. She didn't have that ticking clock, counting down to the end of the summer and the resumption of her official duties. She could…simply sink into the marvel of the heat between them and see where it went. Wherever it went.

It felt like a new sort of freedom.

Assuming, of course, that this moment wasn't all he wanted from her.

Amalia rather thought he would dismiss her and prowl away, leaving her to marinate in how little he thought of her now. She braced herself for his cruelty—knowing full well she deserved it—

It was relief when instead of stepping away, putting distance between them, forcing some kind of conversation or merely offering a sneer as he left her, Joaquin only held out his hand.

Saying nothing, which, somehow, seemed louder to her than if he'd shouted.

And still, there were so many things she should have said then. It wasn't as if he'd been particularly kind to her today. Surely she should address that.

You were anything but kind to him, she reminded herself.

And anyway, she wasn't sure she had it in her to confront him. What did it matter what he said now or what she'd done back then? What mattered was this. This overbright, almost painfully intense connection between them. It had been there from the start. And right now, all she could seem to do was bask in the fact that the years hadn't dimmed it one bit.

So she took his hand.

More than that, she reveled in it as he tugged her up and onto her feet. The feel of his hand around hers once again. The grip she'd never expected to feel again. It was as if he was still holding her face, her head. Keeping her right where he wanted her.

Amalia was a little too invested in him wanting her. She accepted that. But then, the force of Joaquin's wanting could, she was reasonably certain, shift the stars in the sky to make the patterns he preferred. That was what it felt like.

As if, deep within her, she was only stars he rearranged at will.

For a moment they stood like that, their hands clasped together. He still leaned there against the stone wall, his green gaze as demanding on her as his hands had ever been.

She watched a new storm track across his face and held her breath, but then he moved. He tugged her along with him as he walked through the open stone lobby. He led her out the other side from the path she'd walked from the docks and her heart took up a kind of drumming, because she knew immediately where he was headed. Sure enough, they wound down away from the hotel, on a path marked PRIVATE. Down the stone stairs that ran along the cliffs and offered views of the sea, before winding around again to the owner's villa.

Though it was no airy villa built with tourists in mind. It had once been a dungeon, perched perilously close to the water line to give the prisoners something to think about.

Sometimes a man needs something to focus his attention, Joaquin had said the first time he'd brought her here. Though he had been looking at her, not his handiwork. *And if it is not perilous, what is the point?*

Joaquin had transformed the old dungeon, a complicated maze of cells that let the sea in. She had laid with him here, on that altar of a bed in his stark bedroom, staring out at the sea that raged *just there.*

You could have had any one of the villas on the island be the owner's villa, surely, she had said. *Why would you choose a former jail?*

I am the orphan child of nobody at all, he had replied in a lazy voice that had not matched his words. *Nearly everyone I met predicted I would end up in prison. Or worse. The dungeon seems appropriate.*

Not that there was anything particularly

dungeon-like about the home he'd built here, save its historic purpose. He had kept some of the details. The entrance, left intact, was a circular, medieval affair with bars everywhere. It had always made her laugh. Because it was all suitably intimidating, she'd thought then. It suited him, the fiercest man she'd ever met.

It still made her smile today, but that was more nostalgia than anything else. The door opened easily, a testament to the kind of money and attention he poured into every detail. No heaving and squeaking hinges here.

He ushered her inside, and everything was as she recalled it. Cool, stark whiteness everywhere, suggesting an airiness she felt certain none of the original inmates had ever felt. The stone was chilled and hinted of damp and was therefore strewn here and there with thick, richly colored rugs. There was art on the walls, most by identifiably famous artists. And instead of the thick stone walls that had once stood, every outward-facing wall was made of glass.

So that, depending on the tide, sometimes the ocean crashed right there against the walls.

It was still exhilarating, she found, as he led her from one room to the next as if he was on a mission. It was still overwhelming and exhilarating at once to be this close to the might and power of the water.

It still felt like him.

In his bedchamber, he whirled her into his arms, then backed her up. Amalia didn't know where they were headed and she didn't care. That, too, felt like a freedom. Because she was no longer the Crown Princess, duty-bound to put a stop to whatever happened with this man. She was no longer required to marry a man of Queen Esme's choosing, however little they might match her own inclinations.

She was no longer required to be anyone but herself, whoever that was.

Right now, all she knew was that she could not get enough of Joaquin Vargas. That he had tattooed himself upon her years ago, and if anything, the colors of that tattoo were brighter now than they had ever been then. As if time had made the mark upon her all the more vivid.

And only he could see it.

Her lips parted on a kind of gasp as her back came up against the thick stone wall at the far end of his bedchamber, hard and cold. Then he was leaning over her, a dangerous glint in his gaze and that storm in the green of his eyes.

And once more, Amalia thought that too many things were said between them, without a single word being passed.

This close, with the light from the sea and sky outside dancing over them, she found herself studying his face. The years had only made him more beautiful, more astonishingly, bracingly handsome. Maybe there were a few more crinkles beside his eyes. Maybe those sharp, sculpted lines of his face had been drawn by a heavier hand these days.

But he still made her heart flutter in her chest and her knees go soft, no matter what stone he felt she should kneel upon.

Going on instinct, and maybe not wanting to hear whatever he might say next—not now, not when she was lost on that wave of nostalgia and need—she reached up and began to trace the bold lines of his face with her own fingers. As if she intended to sculpt him herself. She followed the line of his brow, then the dark slash of his eyebrows. Down the length of that aquiline nose, then backtracking to trace this cheekbone, then that. Then she moved over that stark mouth of his, all the more sensual because she knew how he could use it.

Finally his jaw, so intensely masculine, making him look not so much like a fallen angel, but the sin that had preceded that fall.

He murmured something dark, too low to hear. And Amalia couldn't tell if she was sad she didn't quite grasp his words, or just as happy that they remained opaque. Either way, she didn't ask him to repeat himself.

And then, once more, he claimed her lips with his.

He kissed her, his hands propped on either side of her head. He held her there against that stone wall with only the seduction and steel of his mouth. His lips against hers, coaxing and castigating, as she lifted her hands to the marvel of his chest. He knew how to make her wild. He knew how to shift, at just the right moment, to make it all deeper. Hotter. To make her press up on her toes and push herself toward him, to tease and tempt her almost beyond reason.

Five years ago he had kissed her like this, on a moonless night beneath a whispering palm tree, and he had taught her what desire was.

And then he had taught her how to beg.

Then, better yet, what a thrill it was to get what she'd begged for.

When he finally pulled away now, Amalia was shaking. Joaquin's gaze was so dark it actually hurt. And she had no doubt at all that they were remembering that same kiss that had changed them both.

Forever, she thought.

There was torment in his gaze then, and she braced herself, because surely now would come a little bit of that cruelty he'd showed her earlier. Cruelty Amalia might know she deserved, but that wouldn't make it any easier to take.

But instead Joaquin only shook his head, then pushed himself away from the wall.

"Take off your clothes," he ordered her, his voice rough. "I wish to see all of you."

Amalia didn't hesitate. She instantly kicked off her shoes and reached for the side zipper on her dress.

And her own lack of hesitation answered a question for her that had lingered, all this time.

It had been the summer, she had told herself in the intervening years. It had been her youth and inexperience. He'd been the first man who had ever really caught Amalia's fancy, and that was why she'd been so abandoned with him. That was why she'd begged and knelt and obeyed his every sensual command.

She had tried her best to shame herself for her reactions to him as each year passed. She'd told herself that she had betrayed her people. That someday, Joaquin could easily hold that summer against her, telling all and sundry whatever salacious stories he liked that would undermine her position on the throne. How could she not have thought of that at the time? How could she have put herself in *so many* compromising positions?

Though she'd always known the answer to that. It was because she'd thought only of him. Only of Joaquin and the pleasure that burned on and on between them.

But even as Amalia had spent many a day lecturing herself for her trespasses, there had been a part of her that had never been cowed. The part of her that had always wanted him, no matter what happened. No matter what it cost her.

Even if it's the throne, that part had whispered sometimes, traitorously.

That was the part that haunted her dreams. Disturbing her sleep almost nightly, leaving her tossing and turning and waking up overheated, her whole body chaotic. She would lie there, panting, tears rolling down her cheeks, while too-hot images chased themselves in her head and weighed her down in her sheets.

She'd told herself for years that she'd built all this up in her head and made it—*him*—into something it wasn't. *Mountains out of molehills,* she would mutter at herself as she tried, and usually failed, to expel Joaquin from her head.

Especially when the Queen had talked strategic marriages.

But now she understood. It wasn't that Joaquin was himself the mountain, though he was certainly no molehill, either. It was this thing between them. This impossible compulsion. This *need.* That was the mountain, imposing and majestic and theirs to climb at will. She might have been young and foolish then, but she was neither of those things now. Twenty-five was only young when a person was aimless and didn't know what to do with their lives—not an ailment Amalia had suffered until recently.

And still, she wanted nothing at all but to please him.

Not because she felt subservient to him in any way.

But because the more she pleased him, the more it pleased her. Deep inside. Physically, yes, but it was so much more than merely physical.

And somehow, he had known that she

needed that, right from the start. Amalia had spent her whole life in the service of others, but had never done so directly. On her knees. In his hands. She had never really understood true service until then. He'd given her that gift.

I don't know why I like to do these things, she'd whispered to him that summer. *I think it means something is broken in me.*

He'd been holding her in his lap in the chair across this very room, having picked up from where she'd knelt before him much as she'd done today. *You're looking at this the wrong way, I think,* he had said.

What other way could it possibly be looked at?

But even as she'd asked that question, she'd had her face cradled against his chest and could feel that same need coiling again inside her. Because it was never enough. No matter what they did, she wanted more. One look at Joaquin had opened up the floodgates inside her and she had doubted very much they could ever be closed again.

She'd been right. They had never closed.

But that summer, she hadn't wanted to think about such things. Because she'd known she would have to return to Ile d'Montagne. She'd known that whatever this was, whatever he'd tapped in her, she would have to shut it off again.

If she could.

You are worrying about what other people might think instead of what you think, he had told her, his chin on the top of her head, holding her there like they were puzzle pieces made to snap together just so. *I suggest you stop. There are no other people in this room,* cariño. *Here there is only you and me and how we feel. Nothing else matters.*

Over time, she'd told herself he'd only been saying that because it allowed him that power over her. But she knew better now. He didn't demand that power over her.

She craved it.

And so here, now, while the surf thundered outside and soaked the windows, Amalia indulged herself.

She didn't question the urges that raced through her, making her blood feel too hot in her veins. Today she was a new woman. Today she was whoever she wanted to be, so she leaned into these things she wanted. Having left her wrap on the floor in the lobby, she thought no more of it as she stood there before him and stripped off the armor she'd worn to leave the palace.

The perfect dress that showed her femininity without highlighting too many of her assets she kicked aside. The strand of quiet pearls she unwound from her neck and let fall. Then she stood before Joaquin wearing nothing but the lacy panties that hugged her hips and the bralette she wore because though her curves were not that exciting, it had been ingrained in her that a lady of stature did not wander about with her breasts uncontained like some common harlot.

But it turned out she might very well be a common harlot, as she was, by virtue of the notably non-blue blood in her veins, common to the core.

She took her time pulling the bralette over her head. Then tugged the lacy shorts over her hips so she could shimmy then down her legs. Only when she was naked at last did she stand, find the green of his eyes again, and then unclip the hair he had messed up, but not undone, so that it tumbled down past her shoulders.

Joaquin's gaze ignited.

She felt as if the world was roaring out the pleasure of this, the tug of this unquenchable need, and only realized when he swept her up into his arms that Joaquin was the one making that sound. But then she realized that she was echoing it, there in the back of her throat.

He carried her over to his bed and lay her out on the mattress, stripping off his own clothes in the kind of haste that indicated he was as swept up in this as she was.

That only made her glow brighter. Hotter.

And watching Joaquin undress himself was a pageant.

She made herself stay where he put her, so she could enjoy the show.

But it seemed as if she only got little glimpses of that flat abdomen, the ridges that climbed from it, and the magnificence of his chest. Because almost at once he was coming down to find her on the bed. To take her in his arms and roll them both around and around, until she was dizzy and giddy and lost, and his mouth was busy on her neck, her breasts.

She wrapped her legs around him and could feel the hardest part of him there against her inner thigh, a thick, long insistence she had already tasted so well.

Her mouth watered all over again.

Amalia thought then that she might die if he wasn't inside her. As quickly as possible.

It was possible she said that out loud.

He paused, reaching out to one of the tables beside the bed and quickly sheathing himself. Then he stretched her out beneath him, gathering her wrists in one hand and holding them up high over her head. She arched up against him, crossing her legs behind him once more, and despite five years of telling herself she would never repeat the shameful things she'd done in this bed, she was pleading with him again.

Begging him.

Again.

"Now, Joaquin. Please, now."

And she could feel the dark curve of his mouth as if he smiled like that inside her, even as she watched it change the shape of his mouth.

He teased her, because he could. He dragged the blunt head of himself through her heat, and laughed at the noises she made.

He made them both shudder.

And only when he was ready, only when he chose, did he lean down, gather her close, and then slam himself home.

Amalia broke into a thousand pieces immediately, digging her heels into the small of his back and holding on as she bucked and shook.

He waited, every part of him taut and tight. He held himself over her as if it took every bit of willpower he possessed to let her dissolve in his arms without joining in. He looked as if it was torture.

Only when she caught her breath did Joaquin begin to move.

And everything was wildfire once more.

Only this time, both of them burned.

His pace was impossible. And glorious.

And far, far better than the dreams that had kept her alive all this time.

All she could do was hold on as best as she was able, wrapping herself tight around him as he took them both on the wildest, most glorious ride of her life.

Her nails dug into his back. Her hips rose to meet his as if of their own accord. Her head was thrown back, she was sobbing out her joy, her need, her dark delight.

And in that moment, Amalia wouldn't have cared if the entire population of Ile d'Montagne was lined up at the foot of the bed, watching them.

Because this was beautiful. And she was entirely his.

It had been that way since the moment she'd laid eyes on him and neither time nor distance nor her role in a far-off kingdom had changed that one bit.

This time, when she shattered once more, she heard his cry as he came with her.

And she thought, as she spiraled off into nothing in his arms, that at least there was this.

Amalia might not be who she'd always believed she was, but there was still this. There was still Joaquin.

And somehow, some way, everything would be all right.

CHAPTER FOUR

JOAQUIN HAD MISCALCULATED.

Grievously.

They spent the day in his bed—and all over the rest of the home he had abandoned when she had left him that summer. When the feast of her body could not sustain them any further, he had fixed them simple meals from the small kitchen he kept here, custom built for those times he did not wish to go to the trouble of walking all the way back to the main part of the hotel.

He had not thought that part through, either. He had spent a lot of time in this place while he was overseeing the renovation of the island. He had been new to wealth then and had wanted to keep an iron control over every aspect of the project. But he had not been that man in years. These days he preferred to control the many teams that did his bidding, not necessarily the projects he had them handle for him.

That was different. When it came to Amalia, however, he was as wholly invested as he had ever been.

He kept telling himself to snap out of it. But always, that same rush of desire would rise in him anew and they would end up back in his bed, learning each other all over again.

Now it was late. Outside the glass walls of the dungeon he had transformed into quiet elegance because it pleased him to know he could do such things, he stood by the window and watch the moon rise over the dance of the waves.

Behind him, the only living creature he had ever loved slept, her dark hair fanned out across the pillow and her cheeks flushed with the force of her dreams. All of him, he imagined. If they were anything like the ones he had of her more often than he liked to admit.

He did not have to look over his shoulder to confirm it. He knew the image would be burned into him forever.

Just like every other image, every other moment.

Joaquin had always intended to taste her again. He was not a man who believed in once-in-a-lifetime events—not he, who could so often dictate the course of both time and events. And lives, come to that.

He had not believed it was possible that he would never encounter her again, and the need to hasten that moment had burned in him. For years. He had liked the fire of it, because he'd been so certain it was hatred.

That it was what she deserved from him after her betrayal. He had taken a kind of pleasure in letting it grow, knowing that sooner or later, their paths would cross again. When they did, he would be ready.

This had seemed too good to be true.

First, that for all the haughtiness she had showed him at the end of that summer—all her talk of her station and what she owed her subjects—she was no princess, after all. He was a mongrel from the streets of Bilbao and yet he had as much right to the Ile d'Montagne throne as she did.

Joaquin knew all too well what it was like to be cast out, mocked and ridiculed, but no one had dared treat him in such a fashion in a long while. It was true that he had taken no small pleasure in the notion that she—so unprepared for these things, so insulated by a lifetime of imagining herself so high and mighty— must face them all the same.

Perhaps that made him as petty as he was

sometimes accused of being. Though he noticed that those who called him such things were always the same people who reaped what they, themselves, had sown.

When he'd found that she actually dared return to Cap Morat, he had felt the way he often did when the world arranged itself to suit him. That all was as it should be. That all was right and good.

He had anticipated wanting her, for who would not want her? Amalia's beauty was exquisite and inarguable. Much had been made her whole life of the delicacy of her features, the stunning blue of her eyes, her innate grace.

All of which, it turned out, came courtesy of a cornfield. Not the royal heritage that was supposed to have produced it.

He had anticipated enjoying all of that, as he always had, because he had been captivated by her beauty once before. And enjoying more, perhaps, that all along, they'd been commoners together here. Despite her attempts to put him in his place.

Now the only difference between them was that he'd earned his money. Hers was a parting gift from the Queen—not her mother—who simply wanted the inconvenient farm girl she'd raised as her daughter and heir to go away. That tidbit had not made the papers yet, but it would. In the meantime, his sources had come through for him.

Joaquin had expected to enjoy that part, particularly.

What he had not anticipated was the *punch* of her.

Even though he knew better this time. Even though he would never be so foolish as to love her again.

The attraction between them was outsize and astonishing, still. He hadn't expected the electricity of it to shock him the way it did. He hadn't expected that merely meeting her gaze would make him feel winded.

He had decided long ago that none of the things he'd thought he felt here, with her, were real. How could they be? He had lost her and he was Joaquin Vargas. He did not lose.

It had not occurred to him that she could be stripped of all the things that had made her who she was and yet still have her own power to spare.

Worse, that she would still have that same power over him.

When he had allowed no one else that kind of leverage. Ever.

Even so, he had expected it would work itself out. He had come to humble her, and he assumed it would be easily done. He would order her to kneel, she would refuse, and he would have the great pleasure of throwing her off his island.

Instead, she had knelt.

He was not sure that he had actually used the brain in his head between that moment and this. Indeed, he knew he had not.

So he stood still. He watched the moon and the sea. And he despaired of himself.

"You look appropriately ferocious for a man who lives in a dungeon half beneath the sea," came her silvery voice from his bed. "Even from behind."

Joaquin did not respond. Perhaps he could not. He heard a whisper of sound and then she came to stand beside him, wrapped up in the sheet from his bed. Making a sheet he had given little thought to, ever, look like the finest garment ever made to caress a woman's form. It looked as if it had been created to pour all over her like that, as if the moonlight had spun itself into silk.

"I'm going to be honest with you about something, though I probably shouldn't," she told him softly, as if this room had become a confessional.

Her gaze was directed out toward the sea, and his chest felt tight, because she looked almost...troubled. The frown he remembered but had not seen in years, in her press appearances or here today, had insinuated itself between her brows again. Her black hair tumbled down her back, looking anything but smooth. For a moment, it was like looking back through time.

Back to the meat of that summer, before she'd turned into a statue. Before she'd acted as if nothing about him or them concerned her at all. For a moment, he could see once more the bright chaos of the younger Amalia he'd known. Not the measured creature, the Crown Princess, who seemed to know too well that anything she said or did could be used against her.

It was unfair, he knew, when that was what he wanted from her. Anything and everything that he could use to do to her what she had done to him.

"Is honesty a factor here?" he asked, his voice hardly seeming like his own. He blamed the moon. "It was not before."

The moon he was busy blaming for his weakness had captured his attention, so he sensed her reproachful look more than saw it.

"I was nothing but honest with you, Joaquin. All summer long, and then at the end, too. Could I have tempered my words? Certainly, and I wish I had. But the message was still the same. There was no possibility that Queen Esme would permit any relationship between us. At the end of the day, what could possibly have prettied that up?"

Joaquin didn't want to touch that. Or maybe the real truth was, he wanted nothing but to touch it. To tear it apart with his fingers. To bellow out the five years' worth of wounded pride and all those other shattered things inside him he refused to accept were there.

He *refused*. "Was this the honesty you meant? I could do without it."

She turned, putting her back to the glass. Then she tipped her face toward him, still swaddled in that sheet, but he saw *her* there. Amalia, as deep in this as he was.

As he *had been,* he corrected himself.

"I had convinced myself that nothing could be as intense as that summer was," she told him, as if she was offering him a confession. And God knew he would take it, especially when her voice was so low, so raw. "I was wrong."

Joaquin looked down at her, though he knew it was dangerous. Her hair was tangled now, messy from his fingers. Just the way he liked it. Her lips were slightly swollen from his, and if he wasn't mistaken, the faint hint of his jaw was all over the tender skin of her neck.

This was how he liked her. Thoroughly debauched, and all his.

But none of this mattered. None of it was real.

"The intensity is the only reason I allowed you to return here," he told her, and even that felt like too much of an admission.

And he was staring down at her face. He could see her reaction.

She blinked, once. That was all.

And then the Amalia he remembered, the Amalia he craved, disappeared as he looked at her. Her face smoothed out, and became serene.

Eerily serene, to his mind.

Something in him turned over at that, because surely that was a loss. Surely that was something less than honesty—though he doubted if she even knew how much she'd changed from that open girl back then, so filled with sunshine and wonder.

But he knew.

"Joaquin," she said, in a quiet voice that matched the sudden steadiness of her gaze. "I hope you know there was never a day—"

He moved then, sliding his palm over her mouth and holding it there as her eyes widened.

As blue as the sea behind her. And as treacherous.

He needed to remember that above all things.

Because he could not allow this. She had been the exception that proved the rule, and she'd proved herself unworthy of it. He had let her in. He had allowed her to see parts of him he hadn't known were there. He had never given anyone else that privilege.

And she had squandered it. It didn't matter why.

Joaquin could not go back there. He could not tolerate her inevitable betrayal once again.

He had grown up hard, but it had been his life. He had never cried about it. He had been far too busy digging himself out of the hole he'd found himself in by virtue of his birth. And it turned out that no matter what all the soft, well-fed wellness gurus liked to say, empires really could be built on spite.

Joaquin had built his that way, and happily. There had been nothing soft in him, ever, until he'd encountered a princess on his island.

She had made him *feel.* Then she had left him. He could not forgive it.

He would not.

Joaquin refused to entertain even the barest hint that they were headed in that direction again. If he could have dug out his heart with his own hands and gotten rid of it, he would have. He did not intend to risk it again.

This was about revenge and nothing more.

He could have moved his palm from her lips, but he didn't.

"There are only two things, maybe three, that I wish you to do with your mouth," he told her with a certain grimness that still didn't manage to cut that same desire for her that burned in him, always. "None of them involve talking."

He felt her smile there beneath his hand, and that did not help. She pulled her head back, so he could see that smile whether he wished to or not. And it did not exactly keep him focused on making this moment work to his advantage.

Because she might have changed in the years since he'd seen her. But she still looked at him as if he was a wondrous, magical creature when he knew otherwise.

"No one has ever spoken to me the way you do," she said, still smiling. Even her eyes were shining, bright enough to rival the path of the moon across the water. "I still don't understand why I like it so much. Or don't hate it the way I should. It was one thing when I was the Crown Princess and you could reduce me to nothing but a half-wild woman with a few dirty words. But now I really am nothing but a woman, and still. It has the same effect."

Joaquin couldn't listen to this. He couldn't engage with her in this way.

Allowing her to talk at all was the problem. He knew that. Because he wanted, still and always, to glut himself upon her. There was no changing that, apparently. There was no pretending otherwise.

But he saw no reason why he should risk *liking* her again. When he looked back, he could pinpoint that as the disaster that had precipitated all the rest. Liking Amalia had been the beginning and the end. When had he ever *liked* anyone?

His life had not lent itself to such luxuries. It had all been about extremes. Living by his wits on the streets, viewing others as marks or possible future marks as he'd set about getting out of Bilbao. And then teaching himself a rudimentary understanding of finance, mostly because he had once encountered a group of hotshot bankers in Madrid who had sneered at him and told him to get a job.

I'll take yours, he had replied.

And so he had. By virtue of buying everything that particular group of bankers had put their grubby fingers in, then firing each and every one of them. Simply because he could.

He had liked every step of the journey. He had liked how easy it was, once he put his mind to something, to make it happen. He had certainly liked firing the men who had thought themselves so much better than him on a city street.

But that was liking things he did. Not who he was.

Joaquin had never had friends. He had allies or enemies, with no in between. And well did he know that a friend one day was often an enemy the next.

He banked on it.

It had not been until Her Royal Highness Princess Amalia had gazed at him as if he was a sheer delight—there on a patio he'd built in the sweet Spanish sun he'd always taken for granted—that he had discovered there was something else.

He hadn't understood it at first. What was this overwhelming compulsion he felt when he was near her? Not merely the urge for sex. He was used to that. He had always had healthy appetites.

It was only Amalia whose *company* he desired.

And look what it had got him.

He rubbed at his chest, annoyed that his heart still beat there. And worse, that he could feel it, as if it was a commentary on his behavior.

Joaquin could not allow this to happen again.

He would not.

"You were a virgin," he told her now, his voice dark. Almost as dark as the sea outside, gleaming beneath the moon. "You do not know the ways that men are with women."

And he could see the hint of a crease appear between her brows. He knew she would argue. Or say something that he would ignore in the moment and then spend the next eternity turning over and over in his head.

So he took her mouth instead.

And he wrested the sheet from her fingers, letting it pool at her feet, before lifting her up and wrapping her legs around him. Because surely, if he sank into her completely—if he indulged himself completely—he would burn this out, whatever this was.

This unwelcome poltergeist of sensation inside him that had never abated.

No matter how he had tried these last few years to blot her out as if she had never existed.

He carried her back to the bed and lowered them both down.

Her sighs were like music. Her taste was addictive.

But he'd already answered the question to his own satisfaction. She'd been a virgin that summer and he had been foolish. Neither of those things applied to this situation. Neither of those things were factors any longer.

He did not have to be careful with her. He could treat her as he had treated any woman, though he rarely allowed them more than a night. Perhaps a weekend, on rare occasions, usually because he needed a date for some or other event in some far-off locale. He always made certain the women he took with him knew where they stood.

If they didn't like his bluntness, he was always more than happy to find someone else.

Joaquin Vargas was known for his business decisions, ruthless and sometimes cruel. He treated women the same way.

And anyone else who happened into his orbit.

That was what he'd learned on the streets. That was how he'd survived.

This would be no different.

Having already made mistakes with her, he would not be so foolish as to repeat them. He would treat Amalia the way he treated any obsession he happened upon. He would give himself to it totally, knowing all the while that soon enough, his obsession would burn itself out.

Maybe then he could be free.

Of this. Of her.

And as he moved over her in the bed, sinking deep into her flesh, and losing himself in that glorious burn, he assured himself that was what he wanted.

Freedom above all else. Because nothing else that he had ever touched had lasted.

Only his freedom to do as he liked, then move on when he was done.

Soon enough, he would leave here again, and he would be free. But this time he would not carry her with him, forever lodged in his heart, in his sex, and too many dreams at night.

Joaquin told himself he was tired of being haunted.

So he set about vanquishing this particular ghost the only way he knew how.

CHAPTER FIVE

THE DAYS BLED one into the next. One week, then another.

It was tempting to imagine she had always been here on Cap Morat, in the shadow of the once mighty fortress. Amalia didn't have to try too hard to feel as if, maybe, she had sprung into life in the Spanish sun and the sweet sea breezes. That this was simply who she was, a creature of appetite and leisure, no end and no beginning.

One morning, she found herself wandering her favorite path. It was the one that wound around the perimeter of the island, ranging from down on rocky beaches to up on higher cliffs, every step offering stunning views. Either of the sea on all sides or of the hotel itself, standing tall on the highest part of the island. Amalia liked that there was nowhere she could go on the island without seeing the old fortress. As if it alone stood guard over her, keeping her past from catching up to her here.

It was a lovely notion.

Joaquin had allowed a skeleton staff back on the island. His half-underwater dungeon had an office suite and he retreated to it at odd hours, barricading himself in there to buy and sell and whatever else it was he did with such ferocity. But when he emerged, he did not always have the patience to make his own meals. It had not been more than two or three days before the kitchen and cleaning staff returned, along with few other key personnel to see to it that Joaquin had every last thing he desired at his fingertips.

Amalia greatly enjoyed being one of them.

She tipped her face up to the sun as she walked, happy that there was enough of a breeze off the ocean to keep her cool. She wore her sun hat, as planned, and periodically had to clamp it to the top of her head with a free hand to keep the wind from stealing it away.

Her whole life seemed to her now, here on this island, as if it had been a dream. Her childhood had been a dreary slog of lectures on responsibility, uncomfortable public events, and her mother's dire warnings about what could befall a young queen if she were not careful. Not that she had ever been given the opportunity to be anything *but* careful.

Then, a pop of color. A burst of light. Life, finally, came for her on this island. She had lived a lifetime that summer. And she'd known it while it was happening. Even then, she'd told herself to hold on tight to every scrap of color and sensation, for she would have to live on it all the rest of her days.

She really had done her duty the day she left here, walking away without looking back no matter how badly she'd wanted to and burying herself in her responsibilities once more.

And now here she was on this island once more. Slowly coming alive again.

Amalia didn't know what it meant long-term. If it meant anything at all. At some point, she was aware, she would have to engage with the world again. She would have to find something to do with herself. She was aware—Joaquin had informed her that the whole world was aware—that Esme had given her enough money that it was not necessary for her to do anything at all. She wanted to think of that as a gift, even a loving gift, but she knew Esme. She knew it was more complicated than that.

If Esme had her way, as Queen, her counterfeit daughter would disappear entirely. What Amalia thought Esme really wanted was to go back in time and not have this switched at birth situation happen in the first place. It was entirely possible Esme had discharged some of her ministers to look into time travel. But in the absence of that, what she'd likely prefer was that the stain that was Amalia—or, rather, the circumstances that had led to Amalia having been raised to imagine herself the daughter of the Queen of Ile d'Montagne—to fade from sight forever. Because the monarchy would go on, and Esme preferred that it do so with as little scandal as possible.

On the other hand, Amalia knew that Esme was genuinely fond of her. That despite everything, Esme likely wished that there was a way she could have kept the daughter she'd raised with her... But Esme was all about her throne, always. She would always put Ile d'Montagne first, even now.

She probably hoped that Amalia would continue to do the same. That she would choose a quiet life, far from the public eye, and live in a way that reflected well on the throne no matter where she ended up.

And there was a huge part of Amalia that wanted that, too. Because she hadn't stopped loving Ile d'Montagne, or the throne, or Esme, just because of a few blood tests. Still, even if she chose that route, if she lived the rest of her life in quiet, elegant virtue, there was still the question of where. And how.

Unfortunately, she didn't think she would be much good at doing nothing, however elegantly or virtuously, despite her time on the island. But here on Cap Morat, she wasn't doing *nothing,* exactly. She was luxuriating. She was engaging each and every one of her senses, immersing herself in the sensual banquet that never seemed to end.

She swam in the pools, as if testing them all to see which one might be her favorite, though she could never make up her mind. The one on the cliff with the infinity pool that made the horizon seem nearly *right there,* within reach? The soft, warmer pools clustered on one side of the hotel, some of them shaded, each and every one its own delight? How could anyone choose? There were also hot tubs at night. One set into the rocks outside Joaquin's dungeon villa, where the ocean waves would sometimes splash over into the pool set into the rocks, an exhilarating punch to combat the heat.

And that didn't begin to address the many beaches she could swim from, if she liked.

When she wasn't swimming, she wandered the island. She climbed up and down all the stone steps she could find, finding every nook and cranny she might have missed last time. And as she did these things, she took great care that when she found herself thinking in the usual endless cycles about Ile d'Montagne, Esme, and her true identity as a farm girl from Kansas, she stopped. She breathed a bit and remembered where she was. Then she tried to put it all out of her mind.

Not because she was hiding from it, but because there was nothing she could do to solve any of those problems here. Because most of those problems weren't her problems any longer, however strange that still was to her.

She swam. She walked. And now that the cook was back, she paused between these activities to eat. And eat. And eat. The cook, she knew, called her cuisine *European*. She took foods from any country that grabbed her fancy. Sometimes she combined it all. Sometimes it was identifiably the food of one country, or another.

And for the first time in her life, Amalia ate with total abandon. Because why should she care if her clothes fit her? Why should she worry for even one moment more about how she would look in photographs? The older she'd gotten, the more she'd fought to maintain a frame that was at least fifteen pounds slimmer than what she would consider her normal size, so that she would appear normal when photographed. It had simply been part of her job.

The part she was happiest to give up, she acknowledged now, while always having dessert. And then, afterward, she napped in the sun, or under an umbrella, dozing off in the afternoons and letting the sun and breeze do as they would.

All of the ways she occupied her time were soothing. And good for her, she thought. But what she did mostly, in and around the rest, was try her best to please Joaquin.

Some days he was harsh, his green eyes glittering and his mouth taut. On those days, there were rules. Tasks he set for her, knowing she would fail them, so that he could mete out his brand of starkly sensual punishment.

She loved every moment of it.

Other days, he was teasing, even playful. He would come and find her in the pools, or out somewhere on the island, and he would take her there. Sometimes he would pull her into a shadowed corner. Other times he would lay her out beside one of the pools, surging between her thighs right there in the open air, which she would never have allowed when she was still the Crown Princess.

But here, with him, she was someone new.

That long-ago summer, she realized now, he had been restrained. He had held himself back, keeping himself on a leash.

He was not doing that now.

Some days, he growled strict commands that she was to stay where she was, splayed out on his bed, only breaking for necessary reasons. And he would visit her, in between meetings, to please them both excessively.

Her head was so full of him—and every last nerve ending, and her skin, and possibly even her very bones—that a full month passed before Amalia bothered to pull out her mobile phone.

It was an unusually rainy day. Joaquin had stormed off to growl at his subordinates after taking out his mood all over her, deliciously. Amalia dashed up the stone path to the grand hotel lobby, where some thoughtful staff member had already lit the great fire. She curled up before it, and powered up her phone, tucking her bare feet beneath one of the blankets on the chair she'd chosen.

"Do you really want to do this?" she asked herself softly.

And the answer was no. She did not. She

was perfectly happy as she was, cut off from the world. But it was a bliss born of ignorance. And she knew that sooner or later, she would have to face reality. Better on her own schedule, she thought.

Even then, while the lock screen of her phone filled with various messages, she held off from looking more closely at any of them. Just for a few moments more.

But an hour or so later, she had deleted all the messages from various so-called journalists. She had checked in with her secret social media presence, restricted only to a very few people she knew personally who were as averse to publicity as she was. And was touched to find that all of them had checked in to make certain she was well.

But what surprised her more was that there were three other messages, all voice mails.

One from Queen Esme, a frigid inquiry into her well-being.

Some might find that off-putting. But Amalia knew the Queen. And knew that for Esme, reaching out at all must have seemed an unforgivable lapse into sentimentality.

Amalia would hold on to that.

The second message was confusing. It was Delaney Clark, her replacement. Or, she countered as she thought that, the real her.

I would love to talk to you, if that isn't too strange, the other woman said. *It's nothing bad. I just know that you spent twenty-five years training for this job, so you're obviously the expert. I'd love to pick your brain.*

Amalia's finger had hovered over the delete button, and she'd urged herself to press it, but…hadn't.

She told herself she wanted no part of the palace, or anything to do with the real Crown Princess. Why would she go back there? Why would she involve herself in a life was no longer hers?

But she didn't delete the message.

The final message was one she was completely unprepared for.

Hello, came an older woman's voice. *This is Catherine Clark. I'm your… Well. I don't know what to call myself. But I want you to know that I knew. I knew when they brought me the wrong baby, and they told me I was imagining things. That I needed sleep. But I knew. I loved the daughter I raised. I love her still. And I don't need anything from you if you don't wish to give it. But I wanted you to know that… I love you, too. And I missed you when you were gone.*

She couldn't have said how long she sat there after hearing that message, her mobile forgotten in her lap as she stared off into the fire. That simple, quiet message had punched holes through her heart. She could feel it, suddenly filled with all those gaps, except other things flooded in, too.

All the memories she'd set aside or stamped out, because there was no point in wallowing in them.

They flashed through her now. Sobbing out her heart in her bedroom at the age of seven or eight, because once again the Queen had dismissed her for being too noisy. Too loud. Too frightfully common. She'd cried until her eyes were dry and her cheeks hurt from all the salt. And she'd wished, fervently, that she had somehow been adopted. Instead of imagining that she was secretly royalty, the way she understood some girls did, she had wished she could be regular. With a sweet mother who loved her, not a chilly queen who was forever harping on her every last act.

Another flash, sitting with a family when she was eighteen and on the cusp of her own schedule of solo public appearances. She and Esme had visited a family gathered around the bedside of their youngest daughter, who had been suffering from a terrible cancer. But none of them had seemed sad. They had been too busy making each other laugh, holding each other's hands, telling one another stories. They had been bright and connected and happy, even in the face of the unthinkable.

Esme and Amalia had sat silently in the back of the car that had ushered them home to the palace. Silent, because no one spoke until the Queen did, and Amalia knew by then it was never worth breaking protocol in Esme's presence. The whole way home Amalia had wondered what it would be like to have a family like that. Where what mattered was that they were together, no matter what.

And all this time, she'd had a real mother. Not a queen. A mother who had called her up, even though they were strangers to each other, just to tell her that she was loved.

She knew Esme would never do such a thing. It would not even occur to her.

If you ask them, a great many commoners have love and happiness, Esme had said once, when Amalia had dared to ask if Esme had loved her husband—supposedly Amalia's father—the late, lamented Jean Philippe, who had died not long after Amalia was born. *What we have is history. A legacy. The purpose of the throne to guide us in all things.*

Can't you have both? Amalia had asked. Too fervently.

Esme had looked at her almost pityingly.

Amalia had been twelve and had been reading books she shouldn't, stealing them from the palace staff and inhaling them under the covers when no one was watching. But all those romantic paperbacks had given her courage. She didn't look away.

At twelve it had seemed a victory.

No, child, Esme had replied coolly. *It is but one of many choices you make in your life. No one can have everything. Only the foolish try.*

Thinking back now, Amalia thought that might have been the only time love had been discussed between them. At the time, she had been distraught, because she understood that Esme was telling her that her parents had never loved each other. But she'd also known that meant it was very unlikely that *she* would be permitted to marry for love, should she ever find it.

But Amalia couldn't imagine why she'd thought love was part of any royal picture, given the fact Esme had never said those words. Amalia hadn't expected she would. *I love you* would have been a weakness, and the Queen was focused solely on making certain her successor was strong and tough. And prepared, for anything and everything.

Love had nothing to do with it.

Yet now Amalia held in her hand a mobile

phone that held a message that proved to her that from across the world, the woman who'd given birth to her had no fear at all of love. And no qualm about reaching out to share it.

She thought she ought to celebrate that. Instead, she felt shaken to her core.

And then, suddenly, it was as if the air changed around her. She glanced up, expecting to find the rain had cleared outside. But it was Joaquin who stood there.

He usually dressed for his meetings, always looking the part of the billionaire CEO he was on his various videoconferences. One day, to amuse himself during what he'd told her would be a particularly boring spate of meetings, he'd had her sit in his office with him, perched where he could see her. She had been completely naked. And from time to time he'd scribbled out directions for her. That she should touch herself this way. That she should move around that way. By the time he was finished with his meetings, Amalia was nearly sobbing with frustrated longing and hunger. And he had taken her right there, tossing her across his desk and slamming his way inside her at last. He had thrust once, then twice, before cursing and pulling out again to fumble a condom into place.

She'd been so ready for him that when

he thrust home again, she'd screamed, then bucked out her pleasure against him while he sought his own lightning-fast release.

The memory alone made her breath catch.

Today he must have spent more time on the phone instead of a video. He wore a now soaking wet white button-down shirt, rolled up at the sleeves, and a pair of dark trousers that seemed to cling to every part of his thighs that she liked best.

"Have you been standing there long?" she asked.

Because there was something about the way he was looking at her. Almost as if he felt haunted.

"Not long," he replied in his gravelly way.

She remembered this from their first summer together. When she had become so attuned to him that she could feel his voice inside her, as if every syllable was a caress against her tender flesh.

Joaquin did not come closer. And Amalia stayed where she was, because she liked to look at him. And today he was wet from the rain, so that shirt clung to him the way she normally did. He looked like every fantasy she'd ever had.

She almost laughed. He *was* every fantasy she'd ever had.

"You look…sad." Joaquin bit off that last word as if it tasted bad.

Amalia glanced down at her mobile, then shook her head. "Not sad. Not really. I think my circumstances require an appropriate amount of introspection, that's all. And I'm new to the practice."

Outside, the rain picked up, beating down hard on the stones. It was so loud she thought it surely could have drowned them both out, had either one of them been speaking.

And still, somehow, the storm in Joaquin's gaze raged louder.

"Everything in my previous life was out-ward-facing," she told him, hardly knowing she meant to speak. It was the way he was looking at her with all of that green in his gaze. It made her feel reckless. "Whatever thoughts or feelings I might have had, about anything, needed to be locked away in ser-vice to my public persona. In case you won-dered, I didn't get to pick that persona. The role was chosen for me and I was expected to fill it. The girl you met here five years ago was…not me. She was an anomaly. An escape from reality."

She saw his lips flatten at that. But he still said nothing, only stood there as if he had braced himself for a fight.

"I'm not complaining," she found herself continuing, though the idea of a *fight* made her blood move a little quicker. "Just a fact. My—Queen Esme is of the belief that while the monarchy holds all the power in Ile d'Montagne, there are also obligations incumbent upon those of us who hold—or held—those exalted positions. The public is owed access to us. Or not to *us,* as such, but these roles we play. She is also of the opinion that mystery is far better than exposure. I don't suppose this is something you would understand. I suspect you are always and ever you, no matter where you go."

She had found that exhilarating five years ago. He had been a force and she had been, perhaps, a little in awe of how *certain* he was. About everything.

Surely you must feel some hint of doubt, if only now and again, she had said once. They had been walking down by the water in one of the island's protected, rocky coves. It had been a hot day, but Joaquin had only seemed to burn brighter in all that sun.

He had held her hand in his, the heat between them always at a simmer. The look he'd sent her way had only set it to a boil. *For many years I could not afford doubt,* he had said. *Now that I can afford anything, I do not see its purpose.*

Amalia remembered thinking, *I wish I could walk through the world like that.* She supposed that when she'd left him that summer, that was what she'd tried to do.

Here, now, she watched his green gaze narrow, slightly. And he nodded. Once.

"And here's a little secret." Amalia pulled the blanket more firmly around her. "I liked playing that part. There might have been certain restrictions on my life, and I found those difficult at times, but the role of the Crown Princess? I enjoyed it. I knew that I could do real good and I worked hard to make sure that was at the center of everything I did. And I worked hard at the public persona, too. To always appear graceful. Compassionate. Pleasant, yet serious. To inhabit opposing extremes at all times, usually in heels, while always remaining just unknowable enough, because the people do not really want to know every last detail of the personification of their government, do they? It's not easy." She clutched the mobile in her hand. "And it turns out that all this time, it wasn't even my role to play. It would be strange if I wasn't thinking about it."

"They say you lived entirely for the crown."

Joaquin sounded as if he was whispering, but that couldn't be true. Not when the rain was still coming down like that outside. It was only that his voice moved over her like a whisper, then into her like a caress. "That you bloomed with adulation and will wither away without it."

"Then I would deserve to wither away." She tipped her head to one side as she regarded him. "If that's the only thing I was, then I ought to be happy that it's turned out it was never my role to play. We're all just people at the end of the day. Aren't we?"

"There are different kinds of people." And again, she couldn't seem to look away from that green gaze of his, and how intensely he seemed to be watching her. As if he was looking for something in particular. "Most of them are weak."

Amalia didn't exactly laugh at that, though a puff of air escaped her lips. She lifted her hand to push her hair back from her face, and only then realized it was trembling. "Everyone knows your story. I don't think anyone can compete with it. Compared to you, there's nothing but weakness in this world."

"You say that, but I doubt very much you know what it means," he said, dark and yet layered through with too much fire. "You have never known what it is to be entirely alone, Princess. No one coming to save you. No one around to care. I could have died at any point during my childhood and no one would have noticed."

Amalia had never heard him put it quite like that before.

"I wasn't sad before." She wanted to whisper his name. She wanted to touch him, comfort him. But she didn't dare do any of that. "But that makes me feel something a lot more than simply sad."

"There's nothing sad about it." He moved then, that rangy, almost rolling gait of his that made her think of how controlled he was. How ready, always, to attack. "Life is only ever about survival. My gift is that I have always known that. I did not learn it later, and to my detriment, like some."

"What you're talking about is *existence*," she said, with a quiet intensity that seemed to come from a new place inside her. "Living is something else. Living involves light, love. Anyone can *exist*. Most do. But it's only when you surrender to life that you get to be truly alive. And that's what matters."

Her words seemed to hang there in the grand lobby, buffeted this way and that by the rain outside and the cold wind that whipped through. By contrast, neither wind nor rain seemed to touch Joaquin at all as he moved toward her.

"And how would you know this?" Joaquin's voice was soft again, but she did not mistake that softness for weakness, not when she could feel the lash of his mockery just beneath it. "You, who have played a role that was not even yours all this time? Is that *alive,* do you think?"

But Amalia refused to be cowed by him. Not today. "I can't do anything about the life that I was told was mine, the one I tried to live as I was told I should." She lifted her chin, and somehow, holding tight to her mobile and knowing the message that waited for her there made her feel stronger. Brighter. "All I can do is make sure that the life I lead going forward is the life I want."

"You should know this by now, Amalia," he growled, and he was standing over her then, his green eyes glittering. "No one ever, truly, gets what they want. Life is compromise—unless you win. And you, I think, were raised to believe you had already won, only to learn otherwise." He shrugged the way he did sometimes, as if nothing could matter. As if nothing ever had. "I do not think the life you have before you is going to be anything you wish."

The life before her that would not include him. He didn't say that, but that was what she heard. Loud and clear.

As if she was just one of his many women, clinging to his trouser leg. She was sure that was precisely how he wanted her to feel.

"I know my life will be exactly what I wish, actually," she shot back at him. "Because I'm not afraid of it. I don't have to conquer everything before me. I don't have to make certain that I win at all costs. The difference between you and me, Joaquin, is that I just want to be happy."

"No, Princess." That was twice he'd called her that today, and the sardonic way he said it made goose bumps roll down her neck. She didn't like it. But then, she supposed that was his point. He was doing this deliberately. So she decided, then and there, that she would die before she gave him the satisfaction of seeing how it got to her. "The difference between you and me is that I know happiness is a lie."

He reached down then and hauled her up and into his arms. The blanket fell off her, her phone clattered to the stone floor, and she didn't care. Because his mouth was on hers and his tongue was stroking deep, making her attempt at defiance seem silly.

When all she wanted was this.

All she really wanted was him.

He spun them around and carried her across the lobby, and she didn't understand what he was doing until she felt the rain fall all over them. Pounding down until they were both soaking wet.

Eventually he set her down on her feet, and a quick glance around showed her that they were out near one of the smaller pools, its surface agitated by the rain that kept coming and coming. Joaquin backed her up until she found the palm tree behind her and she held on as tight she could, her fingers slick against the bark.

He didn't stand on ceremony. It was like the storm all around them was in them, too. Joaquin worked the front of his trousers to free himself, and then he lifted her up, letting her arch back against the palm. Then he slid her down his body, thrusting deep within her.

And every time it felt better.

Every time, she thought there was no possible way the pleasure could be this intense. This beautiful.

And every time he proved her wrong.

She couldn't tell any longer where the storm

was. Inside her, around her. Pounding on her head, pounding deep between her thighs.

Maybe they had been the storm all along.

When she arched up against him, sobbing out her joy into the rain, he let out a deep kind of roar. Then jerked himself out of her to finish on her belly.

Once again, he'd forgotten himself.

And she forgot everything.

"Careful," she warned, in a voice that didn't sound like hers. She sounded silly with lust. Half-mad with passion. Addled by him, again. "One of these days you're going to make me pregnant, and then you'll never be rid of me."

And it wasn't until her feet hit the ground with a jolt that she realized how badly Joaquin was taking that remark.

Because he was looking at her as if she'd betrayed him.

CHAPTER SIX

ONE MOMENT, HE'D been burning so hot he was surprised the rain didn't sizzle as it hit him.

And the next moment, he was chilled to the bone.

"Why are you looking at me like that?" Amalia asked, gazing at him like the impossible temptation she was. Soaking wet, wearing one of those gowns of hers that seemed to envelop her in far too much fabric, yet were almost too alluring to bear.

Out here, in all this rain, the fabric clung to her form, making her seem something more than simply beautiful. It was as if she became something else, something *more*. Some kind of myth, perhaps.

Thank the gods he didn't believe in such things.

"There will be no pregnancy, Amalia," he told her, and it was probably a good thing that she'd called out his shocking irresponsibility.

It was certainly a good thing that she'd done it before he went too far. "Ever."

She stared at him as if he was suddenly far, far away. When Joaquin knew the truth. He was always that far away. He was always *other.* He was always surprised when people failed to recognize the fact that he was not civilized.

Not like they were.

Not like *she* was.

"They call me an orphan, but no one knows if that's true," he told her, the words seeming to come from deep inside him like so much rain. When he never spoke of these things. The stories told about him always glossed this part over. His *humble beginnings.* His childhood of *abject poverty.* Pretty ways to describe a life of grim desperation and too much terror. And he'd certainly never told Amalia much more than the broad strokes, because why would he want her to think of him like that? So weak and small? He felt overexposed already, but he couldn't seem to stop talking. "My parents could be alive right now for all I know or care. If they are, I'm certain they lost whatever humanity they possessed to the drugs and the drink long ago. Maybe they were taken by violence on the same streets where I was left to fend for myself. Whatever the reason, whatever happened to them, it does not take a genius to understand that I possess nothing in me that could ever make a good father."

"If we can only be what our parents were, then I fear we are all doomed," she said.

"I am happy to be doomed," he gritted out. "I thrive under such conditions. But I am not planning to pass it down."

She only stared back at him, clinging to the palm tree behind her as if it was the only thing tethering her to this earth. Joaquin did not choose to ask himself why he found that…a kind of grieving.

"I don't want your confidences," he told her, as harshly as he could. "I don't need you to tell me what it is to *be alive*. I thought I made myself clear, Amalia."

His intention was to devastate her. He wanted to, with a kind of greed that matched the lust he felt for her and made him feel the same intense shame—because surely that would get her to leave him. Because something had to break this fixation, this addiction, and he did not seem able to do it himself.

Surely if he crushed her, she would go.

And he could sink back into the life he'd made for himself, where he was not required to *feel* a damn thing.

He could see her pulse beating wildly in her throat. He could see the way she trembled, there in the rain.

But if he'd expected her to crumble, he was to be disappointed.

Instead, she wrapped her arms around her middle and studied him. Solemn and careful.

"I understand that you have a lot of anger about how things ended—" she began in the same way.

Joaquin let out a bark of laughter. "I was angry five years ago, certainly. But this is not anger, Amalia. This is revenge."

She blinked. "You're…taking revenge on me? And my punishment is…endless sex? Hot and cold running orgasms? Is this how you get back at all your enemies?"

He couldn't say he liked the way she put that.

Joaquin advanced upon her, well aware she did not cower. Instead, she stood taller. Still, he had to lean over her so he could run his hand along the side of her face, then grip her chin. He held her face there, and brought his down close, so they could be no mistake.

So that this moment could stand as an example of what was really happening here.

This moment that could have been a kiss, but wasn't.

Because this was no romance. This was what happened five years after the romance died—at her hands.

"I *loved* you," he threw at her, taking no care at all to ensure he didn't hurt her. He wanted his words to hurt. He wanted them to land the way they did, like bullets into her tender flesh. She jolted, and he liked that. "I would have given you anything at all. Anything and everything. I would have laid it all at your feet. But all you wanted to do was step on me."

She lifted her hand to his and he thought she would try to peel his fingers away from her chin—but if that was her aim, she seemed to get lost in it.

It reminded him of the first day she'd returned here. When she'd looked at him as if he was a ghost, but one she'd come all this way to find.

She was sopping wet now, soaked straight through, and he thought he should have been able to see through her, too. Not just the gown she wore, currently plastered to her every sweet curve, but *her*. He'd spent all this time peeling back her layers, learning how to make her scream, making her beg and cry out for gods who never came.

But he still couldn't read what he saw there in her endlessly blue gaze.

And he didn't see why she should be a mystery like the sea, when he could barely keep himself to the plan he'd made.

Maybe, a voice inside him suggested, *the mystery here is not her—as she meets your demands and shares herself in all possible ways, but you. Who do not.*

Joaquin didn't care for that thought at all.

"You like to make it sound as if it was my aim to hurt you all along," she said after a long, fraught moment while the rain came down in sheets all around them. "I think you know that's not so."

"What difference can it make? It is what happened."

"My hands were tied, Joaquin." He started to shake his head, but her gaze only seemed to grow steadier. "You will say that does not matter, but it does. I'm sure you would like to think that nothing on earth could have stopped you from doing what you liked back then. Or now. The reality is, there was nothing on earth that had any authority over you. There still isn't. I can't say the same."

"That is a weak argument, Amalia."

"I'm not talking about what I owed the

Queen. I'm talking about the fact that my Queen was my mother."

She did pry his fingers from her face then. She held them away from her, though she didn't let go of him. Joaquin should have jerked his hand away. He told himself he meant to do it at any moment, but one moment became another, and he didn't.

He didn't care to ask himself why not.

"I think it might have been easier to defy a government," Amalia said in that same quiet, yet intense way. "A nameless, faceless body. But in my case, we were just talking about my mother. The only mother I had—and the only parent I had left. I had no wish to disappoint her."

He pulled his hand away from hers then, and moved back far enough that the rain could fall between them once more. And wondered what that must be like. To have a mother, or any parent, who cared that he existed—and who might therefore be disappointed in him. He couldn't make the notion take form inside him.

And he blamed her for that, too. "You can make all the excuses you want. I loved you and you left. Not exactly kindly. You can hardly be surprised that things are not the same now, all these years later."

"I'm not surprised at all."

Her shoulders straightened, that little tell of hers that told him she was slipping on that princess mantle once more, and he wanted to hate that. He wanted it to be evidence against her. But instead, he found he admired it—given how many titans of industry trembled before him, it was an enduring surprise that one tiny ex-princess seemed entirely unaffected.

Maybe not *entirely* unaffected, he revised in the next breath, when he took a closer look at the goose bumps running down her arms.

"I was only surprised that, having made it so clear how much you disdained me, you chose not only to come and greet me here on the island, but to stay," she was saying. "Then to clear the island of any other guests so we could reenact some of the best parts of our initial summer. If this is your revenge, Joaquin, it seems far too sweet."

He regarded her for much too long, and not for the first time, wondered how he had gotten himself into this situation. With this woman who could tie him into knots—and did, seemingly with precious little effort. When he was no pedigreed playboy like the titled fools Queen Esme had considered worthy of her daughter. He was Joaquin Vargas.

He had faced down more so-called monsters this year than most people encountered in a lifetime. It was a sport. Sometimes he took a meeting for the express purpose of showing the self-aggrandizing heads of widely feted corporations how little he cared what they thought of him.

He had always been good at claiming the power in any situation.

And he had a flash of clarity then, slicing through the rain and deep into him. That was the trouble here. He kept confusing the issue. He kept letting her think he cared, and deeply. That was what she thought this intensity was.

Really, Joaquin should have anticipated that.

"How many lovers have you taken since that summer?" he asked her, almost idly.

And tamped down, hard, on the instant howling thing inside him that did not wish to know the answer to that question.

Amalia laughed. "Will you be sharing the number of your lovers in return?"

"I cannot possibly count that high," he replied coolly.

And she didn't flinch. Not exactly. Still, something changed, and in its wake, she looked rueful. "I knew that, of course. It's a funny thing, that love you claim you felt for me, isn't it, Joaquin? Because to the casual observer, it would appear that you expressed it by sleeping with every available woman in Europe. Be still my heart."

"But you never claimed to be in love," he reminded her, and his temper was a dangerous thing just then. It took every scrap of willpower he had to keep it within him. To make sure it didn't break those chains he kept wrapped tight around it. Because he shouldn't have had the faintest shred of temper in the first place. She had never told him that she loved him. No one had ever told him they loved him. He was the only fool who had uttered those words. "So I can only assume you slept with twice as many."

"My only lover was my duty to crown and country," Amalia replied, her blue eyes glinting in the rain. "Everything that happened here that summer was out of character in every way. An extraordinary departure from my actual life."

"And yet here you are again," he murmured. "When surely you should have headed straight home to your true motherland. Cornfields, as I understand it. As far as the eye can see."

He had never seen a cornfield. Yet Joaquin

felt certain that the faint hint of derision he used when discussing them was warranted.

Amalia's blue gaze gleamed. "The only thing I know about Kansas is that it has tornadoes. The occasional witch. And farms that end up with ruby slippers, though I've never figured out what they do with all that magic afterward."

He didn't want to dwell on Hollywood nonsense. "All of this makes sense," he said instead. "You still place a virgin's importance on sex."

And he had meant that to insult her. But that didn't mean he liked it when the insult clearly landed.

When she looked as if he'd delivered an actual blow.

"In time, it will pass," he assured her, and he shouldn't have disliked his own words so much. Surely he should have exulted in telling her these truths. In setting her straight. "The more lovers you have, the more you will come to understand that sex is nothing more than a physical release."

She swallowed, hard. He watched her throat move. "And this is your revenge, then. Sexual exposure therapy."

He didn't mean to move closer to her again, then realized he'd done just that. This time he took her shoulders in his hands and drew her up on her toes.

Revenge, he reminded himself. *This is meant to be revenge.*

"I will do whatever it takes to conquer this," he growled at her. "I will not allow you to haunt me. We will stay here, you and I, until you cannot take it anymore and leave. Or until I feel as much when I touch you as I do in any random handshake."

She laughed at that. It was a wild, provoking laugh and he thought she knew that, though she did nothing to stop it.

"How's that working out for you, Joaquin? Because it seems to me that if anything, this *handshake* of ours is only getting more intense."

He would have preferred it if she'd kept her unwelcome honesty to herself.

"It won't last," he bit out. "And even if it does last some little while, it's immaterial. Because there is nowhere for this to go. I won't be falling in love with you again. There will be no accidental pregnancies that link me to you forever. I rarely make mistakes, and when I do? I don't repeat them."

"Joaquin," she began.

He pulled her even closer, making sure that he could get his face even closer to hers, so that this was some kind of mockery of every kiss they'd shared so far. It almost felt the same. That intense, that passionate.

This close to unhinged.

"I won't pretend I don't enjoy this chemistry between us," he told her, almost touching her lips with his. "But the only thing I will ever want from you, Amalia, is your body. Do you understand me?"

"Perfectly," she threw back at him.

And for a moment, they both stayed as they were, her chest rising and falling as rapidly as his. Their breath seemed to saw through the air, disrupting the patter of the rain as it fell.

But it was far too much like all the other things they did when they were touching like this.

He uncurled his hands from her shoulders and stepped away, entirely too cognizant of the fact it was more difficult to do than it should have been.

Much more difficult.

Just as it was to turn on his heel and walk away from her.

He stomped down the path to his little dungeon and in all the time he'd stayed here, it had never felt more like the prison it had been than tonight. Joaquin resented the work he'd put into the place, because he wanted to slam the doors behind him, damn it, and yet they all were too smooth and closed too quietly.

In the bedroom, he stripped off his clothes and made his way into the grand shower enclosure and stood there, propping himself up against the wall as the water poured down all around him.

And he told himself he'd meant every word. He had.

And still, everything in him leaped when the door to the shower opened some while later, when the steam had begun to billow around him.

Amalia stepped in, naked now. Her dark hair swirled around her, already wet. It seemed to call attention to her small, perfect breasts, and the indentation of her waist. He had spent a lot of time in this very shower with his hands splayed out over those hips, holding her sex to his lips so he could hear her cries echo off the tiles while he treated her like a dessert. He liked to prop her up against the shower wall, because he liked the way her fists dug into his hair as he held her up on his shoulders.

It was the only time he knelt before her. And that was fair enough, he assured himself. It was all about sex. That was what he'd told her, because it was true.

It wasn't that pleasuring her pleased him, deeply. It wasn't that sometimes, he thought the point of all of it was afterward, when she was limp and curled around him, sometimes right here on the shower floor. It couldn't be the way she buried her face in his neck, the two of them simply clinging to each other while another bout of their endless passion wore itself out.

It had nothing to do with how he liked to carry her out of here after tasting her so thoroughly, so he could set her on the marble counter and take his time drying her off. Toweling every part of her body, then slicking her everywhere with the soft cream she preferred, so she smelled of night blooming flowers with a hint of spice.

And it was best all round that Joaquin did not permit himself to think about all the times he woke to find the two of them tangled up together in his bed, sleeping so close it was as if neither one of them could make it through the night unless they were touching in as many places as possible.

When he sometimes slept on the hard floors of his various residences, purely to remind himself where he came from. And to make sure he never forgot what real life was like without all the softness he now enjoyed.

Softness led to pain. Those were his earliest memories. He had learned either to keep from wanting anything—or to make sure he could buy the lot of it, so he never needed to worry about losing it.

He had veered from that course precisely once.

She closed the shower door behind her and looked at him, her eyes far too large.

"I keep trying to run you off," he growled at her. "But you won't go."

He shouldn't have said that, but she laughed it off anyway.

"Why should you be the only one using this chemistry of ours for your own ends?" she asked, lightly enough. Though he found he didn't quite believe it. Not when her gaze seemed far darker than that bright summer blue it normally was. "Maybe, Joaquin, I just want to use you for sex. Or is that not allowed?"

"It's entirely encouraged."

And as she moved closer to him, he caught her up, lifting her into the air so she could twine that marvelous body of hers around him. He slid her wet body down the length of his, then sighed a little when she opened one of her hands and showed him the condom she'd brought with her.

"So there can be no confusion," she whispered, and he couldn't tell if that was a challenge or a dig. When he shouldn't have cared either way.

He ripped the packet open with his teeth, and sheathed himself in an easy movement, then lowered her onto his sex.

And he'd told her she would get used to this, but he never did. The tight fit. The perfection of her body holding tight to his. The friction, the heat.

Joaquin took his sweet time lifting her up, then lowering her down. Again and again, until her head was tipped back, her eyes were closed, and she was not issuing challenges any longer.

She was chanting out his name.

He should have been jubilant, he thought later, after he carried her out into their bed and rededicated himself to the task of tearing them both apart. He should have been delighted that they were both on the same page.

And later, when she drifted off to sleep beside him once more, curled into his side as if this was something other than what it was, Joaquin lay awake and stared at the stone ceiling. Then out the glass wall where the sea surged and retreated, again and again.

She had just given him everything he claimed

to want. She hadn't fought him. She hadn't dissolved into tears, or begged him to change his mind.

Was that what he wanted? Was his true aim here no more and no less than to humble her? Was that really who he was?

Because a wise man would set that aside, when given assurances that both he and Amalia were on the same page. No emotions. No future. Just the delirious, delicious madness of the passion between them until it waned.

Surely that would be any day now, he told himself.

Any day at all.

Though perhaps he would have believed that more if he'd thought she really meant it. He found he didn't. He couldn't. He looked at her beside him, sleeping so peacefully, and couldn't ignore the way his heart thumped now.

Because maybe he was more sentimental than he liked to admit. Maybe he had fallen too hard for that artless girl he'd thought she was that first summer.

Some part of him had never believed the scornful Princess she'd become at the end.

And he knew his summer girl would never have agreed to an arrangement like this. She would have sobbed. Her heart would have been broken. She might never have told him that she loved him, but she hadn't had to. He'd known.

It had been in every glance, every smile. Every touch.

And she accepted, lying there, that he didn't like the possibility that none of that was happening now. It was fine if *he* did not fall in love. That was his goal.

But he didn't much care for the hollow feeling inside him at the notion that *she* didn't love *him,* either.

Joaquin found he didn't like it at all.

CHAPTER SEVEN

A FEW DAYS LATER, Amalia returned from a long late afternoon walk to find one of the few members of staff on the island waiting for her at the top of the private path that led to the dungeon villa.

"If you would like to change for dinner," the woman said deferentially, "Señor Vargas waits for you on the lower patio."

"Are you sure?" Amalia asked in surprise. Then flushed a bit when the woman shot her a quizzical look. She knew better than to make personal remarks to people who could not, by virtue of their position, respond in kind. *Friendly does not mean friends,* Esme had drilled into her. "I mean, of course. Thank you. I'll get there as soon as I can."

She hurried down the path, pulling open the heavy front door that always made her shiver a bit for those who'd been locked up behind it, and half expected him to be inside.

No doubt laughing at whatever joke this was, or waiting to pounce and examine her every last facial expression to see if he could discern her actual feelings. Then demolish them.

But the villa was empty. Amalia hurried through her shower, realizing as she soaped herself up and rinsed it all away that she couldn't recall the last time she'd taken a shower by herself. Normally, it was only one more venue to experiment with all that *just sex* they were having.

After he'd left her in the rain the way he had, she had not faced the prospect he'd laid out before her with anything approaching equanimity.

On the contrary, she had cried.

A lot.

Her tears had been indistinguishable from the rain and she'd taken that as a kind of blessing. But she'd still slid all the way down to the base of that palm tree, cradled her head in her arms, and cried.

Because everything in her life had been taken away from her and it didn't matter whether she'd wanted those things or not. She'd spent twenty-five years believing they were hers.

Her mother being one of them.

And yet all the commentary—whether from

so-called news sources, or the Queen's inner circle of courtiers and aides, or even Joaquin— all seemed to be in agreement on one thing. That this was all somehow her fault.

As if she, at three days old, had set out to usurp a throne located halfway across the planet.

As if, a voice had whispered inside her while the rain poured down, *your entire goal during your first summer here was to hurt Joaquin as much as you could.*

When the reality was, she had been so naive that it had never occurred to her to guard herself against him. She had fallen so fast and so hard that it had been all over in a single glance. And the only reason she'd managed to force herself to do what had to be done in the end was because she had been so besotted with Joaquin that she couldn't bear the thought of the alternative.

Which was Queen Esme doing what she could not.

She might have channeled her mother when she'd spoken to him, but she had still been far kinder to him than Esme would have been. Yet how could she explain that to him?

Amalia had been the Crown Princess of a pretty little island that most people treated as if it was a real-life fairy tale. No one would believe, ever, that she hadn't known what she was doing. That she hadn't been fully in control of everything that had happened here.

Deep down, she suspected Joaquin still thought that, too.

And that day in the rainstorm, the injustice of it all had left her heaving with sobs she usually kept locked away deep inside.

She'd cried and cried.

But then, eventually, the sobs had stopped.

Amalia had let the rain wash her face clean. She'd sat there, letting the storm pound into her, and she'd let go of the injustice. The unfairness.

Maybe, she'd whispered to herself, *this is what you deserve.*

Because she hadn't always been a good person, had she? She'd let her mother guide her too completely. Any enemy of Esme's had been an enemy of hers, that went without saying. Esme's opinions, on everything and anything, had been her guide. Even when she'd had the opportunity to act any way she pleased, in a situation Esme knew nothing about and could never know anything about, she'd defaulted to cruelty.

How could Amalia blame Joaquin for refusing to engage with her now when she'd treated him that way back then? Surely if she had half the heart she liked to pretend she did, she would not have been capable of saying the things she'd said to him then.

It didn't matter that she'd hurt herself, too.

Maybe what she really needed to accept was that she'd come here, not because she was after freedom. But because she needed forgiveness.

And maybe the only path to forgiveness available to her wasn't the one she wanted. Maybe she and Joaquin really would throw themselves headfirst into this passion until there was none left, and it would all dissolve into indifference.

Maybe, at the end of the day, that was the best version of forgiveness she was going to get.

That was why she'd gone to find him in the shower that day. That was why she'd simply accepted everything he'd said to her.

And in the days since, she hadn't attempted to provoke him. To poke or to prod for answers she liked, or to get him to admit that the intensity between them meant something. Because even if it did, he didn't want it to.

She supposed after the way she'd treated him, she deserved that, too.

Tonight, when she was out of the shower, she took her time with her toilette. She didn't often get the opportunity to dress here, and she'd missed it. Carelessly romping about in the Spanish sun was all very well, but she also liked the sultry lick of bold lipstick across her lips. The slick of mascara on her lashes.

Amalia knew he didn't like her chignon, so she gathered her hair up in something much looser and more inviting on the top of her head, letting tendrils fall where they would. Then she slipped into a shimmering column of a dress that she had bought on a whim but had never worn to any official function, because it was cut much too high on the thigh, and had no back to speak of.

Queen Esme would not have approved.

And only when Amalia approved of her reflection from every angle did she make her way back up the path. She crossed through the lobby, then headed down again on the other side of the old fortress, heading toward the patio that sat on a cliff out on the edge of the island, offering captivating views of the sea beyond.

They claimed Barcelona was visible on a clear day if conditions were right, though she'd never seen it. Then again, it was possible she'd never looked. She had always been far more focused on what was on the island than what might be around it.

She passed the patio where she'd met Joaquin for the first time, long ago, nestled far closer to the hotel. Seeing it made her smile as she kept going down the path, enjoying the soft evening air as she moved. The pathway was lit with small lanterns throwing off just enough light to make it from one to the next, leading her down a gentle slope toward the cliff's edge.

When she got there, Joaquin was waiting.

He, too, had dressed for the evening, and looked nothing short of commanding as he stood there at the rail at the edge of the cliffs. He was gazing at her as if he'd known the exact moment she would appear.

And as she crossed the patio to his side, Amalia couldn't help imagining what that look on his face might have meant, if they were other people...

As if she needed help to break her own heart.

"I'm surprised you wanted to eat together," she said when he took her hand in one of his and, astonishingly, lifted it to his lips. Her heart flipped over inside her chest, though she tried to ignore it. "I would have thought that doesn't go along with your...stated aims."

"You are here, are you not? I might as well enjoy your company."

But his tone was gruff. His eyes were too green. And something in her chest seem to clutch around the notion that this, somehow, was an apology.

The only one she was likely to get from this proud, hard man.

Amalia cautioned herself not to read too much into it as he led her over to a table that had been exultantly, meticulously prepared for an intimate party of two. It sat beneath a pretty canopy that blocked the breeze and any curious eyes from back at the fortress. Joaquin helped her into her seat, then took his own. And for a moment, she could confuse the odd butterflies in her stomach with the bustle of his staff around them as they poured out the wine, then served a first course, a small whimsy from the chef.

But when they melted off into the shadows again, she was left with Joaquin. And the sea. And the quiet all around them, as if this was the sort of date they'd indulged in that first summer, when sex had only been a part of what was happening between them.

That silly, fluttery reaction inside of her kept rolling around inside her, because this was the first time they had sat at a table like civilized adults since she'd arrived here. She understood that it was deliberate. Looking back, she should have known that from day one. He was keeping everything about sex and happenstance on purpose, when she knew perfectly well that he was capable of providing any experience that might take his fancy.

Five-star dining on a cliff above the sea on a whim, for example.

But somehow, even though she tried what was on the plate before her, she could hardly make sense of it. The only thing she could seem to concentrate on was the turmoil inside her.

Possibly because, here, dressed in the sort of armor she had always used to her advantage before, what was happening inside her seemed far more obvious. Because all the rest of the time they spent together, the only thing she could focus on was that greedy passion that she was certain was the ruin of her.

It had already ruined her. She'd known that for years already.

But she couldn't handle the way he seemed so content to sit there and *brood* at her.

"I think a lot these days about the sorts of things I take for granted that I never would have known if I'd stayed where I belonged," she said. For something to say that cut through all that dark green *brooding*. She waved her hand over the formal place setting before her. "Take something as simple as plates and utensils. I somehow think that place settings like this do not feature heavily on a Kansas farm." Amalia smiled as she said it. "Though in truth, I have no idea. For all I know, the woman who gave birth to me speaks of nothing, night and day, but appropriate table manners for all occasions."

"Table manners are nothing but a gateway," Joaquin said, as if he was handing down judgment.

He lounged there across from her, toying with his glass of wine, and his green eyes seemed to burn straight through her. "There's nothing the upper class enjoys more than the hoops it creates to keep upstarts and commoners out of its ranks."

"I tried a similar argument with one of my governesses when I was small." Amalia lifted her own wine to her lips to taste it, not at all surprised to find it was spectacular. "She was unmoved. And made me sit with a heavy book on my head to improve my posture while thinking about the error of my ways."

"I took a relatively high-class lover after I made my first fortune," Joaquin told her, as if this was the sort of thing they discussed all the time. So casual. So sophisticated. His *lovers.* She took a rather larger gulp of her wine. "She was a mistake for many reasons."

"Oh, by all means, enlighten me," Amalia replied as nonchalantly as possible, because she was certain this was some kind of a test. She had romantic feelings for him, as they had both agreed she wouldn't, and so, surely, she would react badly to details of his legions of other women. And in truth, it felt a lot like tearing off a scab to lean forward and smile encouragingly at him, as if what she really wanted was a close, personal tour through all the women he had loved before her.

She had to hope that *love* in this context was nothing but a euphemism. Not that it really made her feel all that much better to imagine Joaquin involved in the kind of wild, passionate acts they'd experienced together— but with someone else. With a great many someone elses.

But he was studying her face far too closely, and Amalia would throw herself off the cliff in front of them before she'd give him the satisfaction of seeing how this hurt her.

"She was like most of these high-class girls," he said with a certain casual disregard that set her teeth on edge. By design, she was certain. "You know how they are. Wholly unaware of how lucky they were to have been born into their position. Always so bored, for some reason, when the whole world is right there at their disposal. And, of course, deeply selfish in bed."

She had been prepared to be quietly outraged and outwardly impassive. But Amalia found herself frowning at him instead. "I don't think I know what that means."

His green eyes gleamed. "Do you not?"

"As you pointed out, so memorably, you are the only lover I've ever had. Am I selfish? Are you? How would I know?"

His gaze grew more intense and he leaned forward, reaching over to take her hand in his. And even that made her pulse leap. Even that made her body shiver into readiness, because she was so attuned to him now that all he needed to do was look at her in a certain way and she would simply *ignite*.

"One of the things that astonishes me about you, Princess, is that no matter your cruelty when it suits you, you are anything but selfish," he told her in that roughly stirring way of his. "Particularly in bed. And that is what many people do not understand. Good sex has nothing to do with tricks or positions. It is about pleasure. And a certain generosity of intent."

Amalia felt herself get warm. Everywhere. "I had no idea you were such a…master of the form."

She saw a flash of his teeth, that hint of a smile that made her feel almost embarrassingly giddy. "I think, Amalia, that you know very well that I am."

He let go of her hand to sit back in his chair again, still smiling while she turned pink all over. And stayed that warm, despite herself, when he kept telling his story.

"She was very boring, of course, this heiress," Joaquin said, as if that was obvious. As if heiresses in his experience were expected to be boring unless they proved themselves otherwise. "But useful. Like many of her ilk, her primary purpose in life was to irritate her father. And like most of them, she is now married to the tedious man her father chose for her, but only after having tortured her whole family with her terrible choices. Like me." He smiled, but this smile had more of a razor's edge. "She used me for her own ends. I used her for polish. Everyone likes a diamond in the rough, Amalia. But only because it is a diamond. It is not the rough that appeals."

"You seem so…unabashed," she replied, still warmer than she ought to have been, given the subject matter. "I was under the impression that most people at least *pretend* that the heart is what leads them."

"Some pay for school. Some have tutors." He shrugged. "I chose my lovers wisely."

"Not everyone can be so wise," she said, and realized she sounded far more wistful than she should have.

"Queen Esme did not make a list of marriageable suitors for you because she liked them." And there was that steel in his voice again, then. "Or because she thought you would. All of her choices were strategic, always. For the benefit of Ile d'Montagne, not you."

Amalia felt a bit less warm and pink, then. "Yes, but I was—"

"The heir to the kingdom. I am aware. I did not have the good fortune to be born so well situated." He didn't say that with his usual dark undercurrent. Perhaps that was progress. "I did not intend to allow myself to be locked out of anywhere I wished to go. Or anything I wished to do. If I have a secret weapon, as my enemies are so certain I do, it is this. As soon as I identify something I need to learn, I dedicate myself to learning it. My adversaries will always think they have one upon me, with their fancy schools and their pedigrees and their silver spoon friendships from the cradle." Another shrug. "I certainly don't need to give them ammunition because I don't know which fork to use."

She mulled that over as the staff returned, taking away her untouched plate, and replacing it with another one, heaped with another demonstration of the chef's prowess. But still, she wasn't hungry. She watched instead as Joaquin picked up what was inarguably the correct fork, and dug in.

Really, she ought to do the same. "What happens when you've conquered all the things that need conquering," she asked him instead. "Do you even have a plan? Or are you simply trying to own as many things as it is possible to own before you die?"

"Only people who have never had to worry about money," Joaquin said, very quietly, "imagine that gathering it is not an end in itself."

"I suppose this is where, like all the lovers you had and disdain, I should apologize for the accident of my birth. Or rather, the proximity of my birth to that of the actual heir to the kingdom of Ile d'Montagne. An accident twice over, it seems."

"But that is the trouble with apologies, Amalia." She was caught, again, in that flash of impossible green. "Who is it that they really serve?"

He returned his attention to the meal before him as if he had merely commented on the weather. Amalia did the same, staring down at her plate and then eating the food there—also with the correct utensils—though she could not have said what it was.

Because what was clear to her, finally, was that there was no forgiveness to be found here. She suspected he might even know that was what she wanted. What was obvious to her, at last, was that he had no intention of providing it.

This was a man who had dated women he didn't like so he could learn *table manners*.

Really, what had she expected?

Amalia suddenly felt remarkably old, then. Exhausted, perhaps. Because she had loved him and lost him once, and that had changed her life. She had gone on as she always had, because that was what had been required of her.

But she had never been the same.

She had spent a lot less time wishing she could be normal, whatever that was. She had focused much more intently on living up to her mother's expectations, partly because she had known—even if Esme had not—that

Amalia had already let her down. But also because she had left Joaquin to be what her mother expected her to be. She had left him, and badly, so that she could be the most perfect Crown Princess the island had ever seen.

Having lost so much, how could she possibly give the life she'd chosen anything but her all?

Now she'd lost that life, too. And she still couldn't have him. Not the way she wanted him. He would never forgive her. Never.

And Amalia did not think she had it in her to be nothing but a cautionary tale he would tell someday, about his *lovers.*

"This was not my finest idea," he said over coffee, when their meal was done. Done, though Amalia had hardly tasted a thing. "I'm too used to having you. Looking at you across a table is torture."

Because the only thing between them was sex, as far as he was concerned. Why couldn't she accept that? Why did she keep imagining it could be different? Joaquin wasn't the problem. He had been perfectly clear.

She was the problem.

And even knowing that, she wanted him. In any way she could have him.

"There are many kinds of torture," she said,

which was perhaps unwise. She made herself smile when his dark brows rose. "Look at where we sleep every night. It's a wonder we can rest at all, with all the things that must have occurred within those walls. You do know they call it the Spanish Inquisition, do you not? That's for a reason."

He laughed, surprising her, when everything within her felt dire and fraught. "And here I thought you slept untroubled by anything. I blame myself. I must dedicate myself to tiring you out."

Sex, she thought again. *Always sex.*

It was really almost funny. Amalia had spent all those years dreaming of things like this each night. And now that she had him a thousand ways a day, she wanted…something else. Something more.

Not because the sex wasn't good. The trouble was that it was earth-shattering. Life-altering.

But he pretended it wasn't. He pretended it meant nothing.

When she could still remember too well how it had felt when he had openly adored her. When she had been so heedlessly, so recklessly in love with him and he had treated her as if she was rare and precious to him.

And there had been a little too much *nothing* in her life lately. Finding out she was nothing, for example. Then being treated like she was nothing by the entire world.

Now, this. More nothing.

Amalia wanted, more than anything, to be something. To be *someone*.

It didn't matter who. She just wanted to be *someone,* at last. And important in some small way to someone else.

And when she let herself think that, it seemed to take hold of her. It seemed to roll through her, marking her, shifting things around inside her. It made her understand, for better or worse, that it might be the one thing she wanted more than him.

"You're looking at me strangely," Joaquin said, and she wondered how long she'd been sitting like this. Staring at him and wishing things could be different. "It is as I thought. We are not meant to sit about making conversation, you and I. We have better things to do."

"What if I set you a challenge?" Amalia set her delicate coffee cup down, with a decisive click of the cup against its saucer. "Just a small challenge."

"To what end?" he asked, because he was always the businessman. He was all about angles and inroads, and the best possible way to get the most while giving very little.

She supposed she had always known that, too.

"There's no end, Joaquin."

She paused a moment, because she felt as if she was poised on a precipice, and not because this patio sat on the top of a cliff. Not because she could hear the sea against the rocks down below. But because of him.

He might think the time they'd spent together was a physical release, nothing more. Weeks upon weeks of it.

But she knew him. In ways she had never known another human being.

And she understood the world in a different way now, too. All the things she'd watched, or read, or heard talked about. All the ways that people interacted with each other, where sex infused everything. Looking forward to having it, wishing they had it, missing when they'd had it before. The world spun around and around the axis of sex, and it was impossible to think about it at all without realizing how profoundly it affected everyone who partook.

And yet men like Joaquin wanted to stand about and claim it meant nothing. That it was like going to the gym and getting a sweat going, if that.

Amalia fully comprehended that this was little more than a distancing attempt on his part. She even understood why. She had hurt him. He wanted to hurt her, and even better, keep from feeling anything for her again.

But she was here. She was taking part in all of this meaningless physical release with him. Joaquin might have thought that he could hide himself there. He couldn't.

The fact was, physical intimacy was intimacy whether he liked it or not.

Bodies couldn't keep up this kind of sustained connection without forming other connections, too. She wasn't as naive as she'd been when she was twenty, thanks to him. So she knew that just because it was intimacy— emotional as well as physical, after all this time—that didn't mean he was going to admit that they were having the relationship they were having.

It also didn't mean she was required to pretend they weren't.

"What if we didn't have sex?" She threw that out there with remarkable calm, when inside, she shook. "For a week. Or even a day. Just to see what happens."

He looked at her for a long moment. Too long. She saw a kind of knowledge in his green eyes that she didn't want to admit was there. As if he knew exactly why she was asking this question. And more, what it would mean to her if he agreed.

"Why would we do that?" Joaquin asked with a soft menace she desperately wanted to mistake for something else. But couldn't. "Sex is the only reason we are both here, Amalia. As well you know."

There was a finality to that. A certainty that she'd missed before. Or maybe she just hadn't been able to take it on board, too concerned with her own shortcomings. Too worried about whether or not he would ever forgive her.

He wouldn't. Because he didn't want to. And that was that.

At long last, Amalia let that settle in on her. She let it take root. And she had been through a whole gauntlet of discovery over the past few months. Mostly she'd discovered that she was nothing and nobody, despite having been raised to be a very specific somebody, fulfilling a very precise role.

This was different.

How could she willingly, knowingly subject herself to life without any hint of love when she was suddenly free to have any life she wanted? What was wrong with her that she *wanted* to stay here with a man who actively and only wanted, if not to hurt her, then to make certain she never, ever felt comfortable with him? A man who had made it clear in a thousand ways that because of what happened before, she could never deserve any better from him?

Why, after everything she'd gone through, was she signing up for this already long-lost battle?

I wanted you to know that I love you, too. And I missed you when you were gone, Catherine Clark had said in that voice mail.

Across space and time, she was loved. As she was not loved here. And maybe it was time Amalia went and looked for love where it was offered.

It sounded so simple. Maybe all these games of princesses and billionaires had confused the issue. It was time for cornfields, ruby slippers, and the one person on this earth who didn't seem to have the slightest bit of trouble claiming she loved Amalia.

She didn't know why she'd waited so long.

"You don't have to do it, of course," she said now. She met his gaze and held it. She did not whimper. Or cry. "But I'm tired of sex, Joaquin. I'm tired of physical releases and nothing else." *And you,* she wanted to say, though she wasn't that brave. Because it wasn't precisely true. Like everything involving Joaquin, it was more complicated than that. "I'm going to Kansas."

CHAPTER EIGHT

AMALIA WANTED TO cry out something like *There's no place like home!* as she made her way along the country road, then carefully turned into what she hoped was the correct drive that would lead to the Clark farm.

She was in Kansas. And she had loved *The Wizard of Oz.* It would be lovely to think of herself as some kind of Dorothy, finally waking up to the place she truly belonged.

But it didn't feel like home. It felt alien and strange here, flat and unwelcoming.

Then again, that might have been her emotional reaction to leaving Cap Morat and Joaquin once again.

He had not made it easy.

The first thing he'd done was laugh.

You're tired of sex, are you? he'd asked her, still there at that table on the top of a cliff. *Shall we test that theory?*

And she would have liked to say that she

had held steady. That she had stood firm in her resolve. That she had stalwartly refused to allow him to reduce her, once again, to nothing but that wildfire that forever burned between them. Nothing but lust and need, forever.

But she was not that strong.

She wanted him too much.

He had taken her there, right there on the table where she had barely tasted her food. But she tasted him. There was nothing better, nothing brighter. He'd swept what few dishes remained aside and made her scream out her need and her fury to the stars above.

Recklessly. Heedlessly.

He'd made her do it again and again.

I told you that you can leave whenever you like and I meant it, he had said, his mouth against her neck. *You are welcome to leave this island at first light, Amalia. I will call for a boat myself.*

She had waited, still splayed out beneath him, because she somehow did not trust this…helpful attitude on Joaquin's part.

Sure enough, his eyes blazed as he pinned her there beneath him with all that green. *But if you leave now, you can never return, Amalia. This is not a safe space for you.*

She'd sat up gingerly, as if she expected

something to hurt, though nothing ever did. Maybe she wished it would. If it hurt, then maybe it would mean something after all. At the very least, maybe it would teach her a lesson she desperately needed to learn.

Thank you, she'd said, because it didn't hurt at all. Sensation swirled inside of her, the way it always did. She wanted him all over again, the way she feared she always would. *That has been perfectly clear for some time now.*

The next day, she expected him to intervene once again. To use her body against her, simply because he could, but he didn't. She woke alone in that bed beneath the high tide line to find her things packed. And even though that really did hurt, and the hurting was not better, she had decided to take that message at face value.

He really had called her a boat. She had taken it to Barcelona.

Once again, while leaving him and Cap Morat, she had not looked back. There was no need—she doubted she would ever get all the images of what she'd done there out of her head. And she already knew she took the ghost of him wherever she went.

Why bother looking back?

It had been simple enough to hire a plane

once she reached Barcelona and fly herself to Kansas. Simple, but not easy. Because she had spent too long indulging her every whim on that island. She felt addicted to Joaquin, strung out on his touch, and it was worse this time. It had been bad enough after that first summer. But at least then she had been filled with purpose when she'd left him. She'd had her work to throw herself into, her role in the kingdom, a place in history. A future to work toward, like it or not.

Now all she had was the slender hope of *love,* of all things, from a woman she'd never really met—except as a newborn. In a place she would never have visited. As a stepping-stone to a future she still couldn't quite envision.

Amalia really did want, so desperately, to feel some sense of belonging here. To feel tugged back into the embrace of this land that had made her, but she didn't. She was grateful that Esme considered knowing how to drive a vehicle essential knowledge, because otherwise, she wasn't sure how she would have gone about hiring herself a car and drivers so far out in what seemed to be the middle of nowhere. Even so, driving felt treacherous out here where the flat land went on forever, so that the horizon seemed both impossibly far away and on top of her at the same time. The sky was too large here. The fields too secretive, somehow—though she suspected that was only because she couldn't identify all the crops she saw.

She eased the little hired car down the lane, wincing every time the dirt track gave way and the tires dropped down with a tooth-rattling jolt. But she'd checked and rechecked, and this was the address Catherine had given her.

Amalia had seen images like this her whole life. It was impossible to grow up anywhere, she imagined, without some notion of the American heartland stamped into her brain. Green stalks of corn. Golden wheat. Whatever the other crops she'd seen were, all in neat lines, rolling on forever. But it was one thing to watch a show. It was something else to find herself in the middle of it.

When she got to the end of the lane she was confronted with an actual American farmhouse to one side, an honest-to-God red barn straight ahead, and the fields of corn all around—hemming her in a bit, she thought. She hadn't really expected the corn to feel like a living wall. But Amalia blew out a breath and told herself that she was no coward.

Even if, at that exact moment, she felt the surely cowardly urge to turn the car around and drive away. As fast as possible.

She pushed open the car door, forced herself to climb out, then stood there, waiting for a sense of homecoming to sweep over her now that she'd arrived at the actual family home where she should have spent her childhood. To make it clear that she had made the right choice. To make all of this feel right.

But instead, she felt profoundly alone. There was only her beneath an endless blue sky above and the corn, watching her as she stood there, trying not to feel dizzy.

Despite herself, she missed Joaquin.

And Amalia hated herself for that weakness. How could she miss a man who didn't really want her? Or wanted her, but not in the way she needed him to? And yet even as she thought that, her body knew she was thinking about him and shivered with that same unutterable delight it always did.

Even here, a world apart from him after she'd left him *again,* she couldn't even work up a decent temper. She couldn't force herself to fall out of love with him, or want less from him, or stop feeling all of these things that would get her absolutely nowhere.

She just wanted him the way she always had. The way she supposed she always would.

And maybe someday, that would feel like less of a life sentence.

Because at the moment, she would have given anything to press her face into the crook of his neck, say nothing at all, and let herself believe that the way he held her could mean anything she wanted it to. That she was precious to him. That he would hold her forever. That what they were to each other meant more to him than a story he could tell over dinner one night.

Amalia jumped guiltily when she heard a noise. She turned to see an older woman step out from inside the farmhouse, letting the screen door slam shut behind her.

And she knew.

Maybe because there was no reason for any other woman to be staring at her like this, but she thought it was a little bit deeper than that. A little bit more.

This woman was her actual mother. And Amalia knew it. On sight.

After so much nothing, she had to admit that it felt like *something*.

She moved, jerkily, around the front of the car. Then she made herself walk across the yard toward the stranger. The stranger who was her mother.

Amalia hadn't known how a person was meant to dress to meet her mother for the first time. As an adult. She also hadn't known what a person wore on a farm. So she'd gone ahead and winged it, going for jeans and trainers and what she hoped was the sort of T-shirt that everybody wore. Instead of it being the kind of T-shirt that only people like her wore while swanning about, trying to seem *relatable,* which wasn't at all the same thing. That she was a fish out of water in every respect would be all too noticeable, she feared—

And worrying about her attire was a lot easier than worrying about all the rest of it.

But when she came to a stop just below the step the woman stood on, Catherine Clark, her *mother,* didn't appear to notice what Amalia was wearing. She was too busy staring at her.

At Amalia, as if she couldn't quite take her in.

As if Amalia was what mattered. As if she was the only thing that mattered.

"Here you are," her mother whispered. "Finally."

And it was possible they stood there for

a lifetime. Maybe two, just gazing at each other. Both of them, Amalia was sure, were cataloguing the other's face. Looking for clues or possibly recognition. As if each of them was a treasure map.

And any other time, simply standing and staring at another person would have been awkward. Uncomfortable. But not today. Not with Catherine.

My mother, Amalia thought, in wonder.

It was only when Catherine came down from her step by the door, that Amalia even noticed that she'd reached out to grip Amalia's hand.

Had she been doing this all along? Amalia didn't know. But she found she didn't mind.

Just as she didn't mind when Catherine led her out into the fields, away from the farmhouse. Straight into the stalks that had seemed like a wall to her. It seemed to Amalia that they walked forever. The corn rose all around them and seemed to whisper as they passed, but Catherine kept walking until she reached a small clearing.

When she stopped, she smiled, and Amalia found herself smiling back. As if she couldn't help herself.

"When I was pregnant with you I used to come out here," the older woman told her.

"I would lie down on the ground, put my hands on my belly, and tell you how your life was going to be. We couldn't see the whole sky but what we could see was blue and beautiful, and I wanted your life to feel that way. Endless possibilities, in or out of the cornfields." She smiled at Amalia fondly. So fondly that Amalia was taken back.

Because Esme didn't do *fondly*. And Amalia understood why. Esme hadn't been raising a daughter and hoping for the best. Esme had been preparing a ruler to take over the country she had dedicated her life to.

And still, on balance, Amalia found she quite liked *fondly*. She wanted to return the favor. She gripped her mother's hands and she smiled back.

"I have—I *had*—a good life," she said, because wasn't that what any woman would want to hear from the child she'd unwittingly given away? And the bonus was, it was true. Being away from that life for a little while had made that even more clear. "A very strange life, I suppose. But a good one. I know what people say about Queen Esme, and it's true that she can be quite formidable. But she loves me. And though I think she would never admit it, because she can't admit such things without appearing

weak, this has all distressed her. Deeply."
She squeezed Catherine's hands. "I have no
complaints. The life I was brought up to lead
was a good one. I loved my work. I adored
my people. I loved the Queen, my mother.
It wasn't always an easy life, but it was a
good one. And now I get to do what very
few people get to do in this life, and create
an entirely new one."

She realized as she said these things that
they, too, were true. That she had gotten
lost in the things she'd given up and a man
who couldn't love her. When all along, it
had been a distraction from the real gift,
which was this. Getting to stand here, looking into the eyes of the woman who'd carried her within her body. And knowing that
whatever happened next, Amalia would be
the one who chose it.

If that wasn't freedom, she didn't know
what was.

"I can't pretend to understand the doings of
queens and princesses," Catherine said after
a moment. "But it brings me great joy to hear
you did not suffer. And that these recent rev-
elations have not wrecked you."

"They felt as if they might," Amalia
admitted. And then, emboldened by the
compassion in the other woman's gaze, con-

tinued. "I'll confess that I used to dream about having a normal life, but that didn't mean I actually wanted one."

"I understand," Catherine said, with a wry sort of smile. "There are few things on this earth more complicated than a wish granted."

Amalia supposed she would know, and better than most.

"But we are all so lucky now," she said, because she wanted to believe that. "Your daughter and I have two mothers each, just as you and the Queen each have two daughters. I suppose that makes us all family."

"And you and Delaney a kind of sisters." Catherine smiled. "For only the two of you can understand both what you've lost and what you've gained."

"This all sounds very wise and knowing and well-adjusted," Amalia said with a laugh. "I hope to fully believe all of it, someday."

Catherine's smile deepened. "I believe you will. And if I may offer a suggestion as you move from one life into a new one, as I myself have just done....?" At Amalia's questioning look she forged ahead. "When Delaney left for Ile d'Montagne, I left the farm as I'd wanted to do since her—since *your* father died before you were born. I thought I might sell it to the neighbors then, but as Delaney pointed out to me, the land is yours. You get to decide what to do with it. In the meantime, I've been building a life for myself in town. I would tell you I love it, though standing here, surrounded by so much history and so many memories, I feel the tug to return. Though I know I won't. My time here is done."

"If you have advice on how to bridge two worlds, I would love to hear it," Amalia whispered.

Catherine looked at her for a long moment, then beckoned toward the ground. Holding Amalia's hands, she took her time kneeling down. She sat for a moment, then lay back the way she'd told Amalia she'd done long ago. Then she waited while Amalia, who had not been raised to clamber about on the ground under any circumstances, did the same.

And perhaps it was foolish to feel a sense of liberation as she stretched out in the dirt, but she did. There would be no one to comment on what she was doing here. No one to take pictures of her in dirty jeans and a muddy T-shirt, then write snide headlines about it in the morning paper.

She could simply lie there, looking up at

the perfect blue sky framed by the stalks of corn as they reached for the heavens.

It was peaceful here. Protected, yet isolated.

"I can see why you came here," Amalia said softly. Two black birds flew overhead, making rough, croaking noises at each other, as if they were agreeing. "Thank you for bringing me back here. With you."

Next to her, Catherine made a little sighing sound, then reached over and took Amalia's hand again.

"Love," she said, with the sort of gravity that lodged itself inside Amalia's chest. Right where it hurt. "Love is what matters, Amalia. The world will conspire against you. It will tell you that you must be practical. That you must contain it, hide it, make it palatable. But love is not meant to be hidden away. It is a gift, in any form. In every form. I lost your father before you were born, but I have loved him every day since. It's a *gift*." She squeezed Amalia's hand. "Whatever you do, you must do your best to never squander love, no matter where you find it."

And all told, Amalia spent two weeks in Kansas.

They stayed in the farmhouse, both of

them, perhaps, needing to marinate in what could have been.

Catherine told her stories. Of her father, who she had loved so deeply. Of her grandmother, who, Catherine assured her, would have loved Amalia excessively and as far as Catherine was concerned, did so now from above. Amalia learned all about the Clark family, tracing them all the way back to when the first Clarks had left Ireland long ago. In return, she made her mother laugh and laugh with tales of palace protocol and the secret language of clothing choices, according to the ever-watchful press.

They would sit before the fire in the evening and exchange their stories. And at the end of each evening, Amalia would climb up the narrow stairs and find her way into a neat little bed, tucked up beneath the eaves. And dream about the life she might have had, right here in this pretty little place where life was simple—which wasn't to say undemanding. Because Catherine also told her why she'd decided to move off the farm. The demands of livestock, crops. The tether she had felt to this land, like it or not, through good years and bad, ups and downs, and everything in between.

But mostly, Catherine spoke of love. In

different forms. The love she felt for the daughter she'd raised. The love she said she felt, here and now, for the daughter she'd carried. The love she felt for her own mother as a dutiful daughter who had not always agreed.

The love she felt for her husband, lost too soon and never forgotten.

When the two weeks were up and they agreed that it was time for Catherine to return to her new life in the aptly named town of Independence, Amalia knew that she would return. Often.

And not only because she'd decided not to sell the land.

She'd agreed to an arrangement with Catherine's closest neighbor, who would tend the land and the crops and claim all but a small percentage of any yield, thereby expanding his operation. Amalia also hired a caretaker for the farmhouse, the barn and the things that went with it—like the vegetable garden—because these things were what made the land a home. Delaney's home, she knew. The place where Delaney and Cayetano Arcieri had honeymooned, though that was hard to believe. Amalia could not imagine the ferocious warlord of Ile d'Montagne in *Kansas*.

But she could preserve the sweetness of this place for the children Delaney and Cayetano would certainly produce, all of them heirs to the Ile d'Montagne crown—and better yet, all of them grandchildren Catherine would claim as her own.

Making them their own kind of cobbled-together family after all. Amalia was happy to do her part.

And besides, she wanted the opportunity to lie in that cornfield again, and lose herself in the sky.

She left Kansas feeling far richer than when she'd arrived. And maybe that was why she took her mother's advice, like the dutiful daughter she'd always been to the Queen, and went to London.

In contrast to Kansas, all bright skies and sunny days this time of year, London was cold and damp. She wrapped herself up tight in the same wrap she had once thrown on a hard stone floor to kneel upon. Amalia fancied that if she concentrated, she could almost find Joaquin's scent clinging to the soft fabric, teasing her.

But then, his ghost had been with her the whole time she'd been out there in those fields. It was a place he had never been, and yet she'd been certain she heard his voice on the breeze. She slept alone, and yet she'd woken in the night—every night—convinced that she could turn over and find him lying there beside her.

One afternoon, while Catherine had napped, Amalia had walked out into the fields on her own. She'd let the stalks of corn whisper to her as she made her way along. She'd followed the directions of the bossy crows, undeterred by any scarecrow.

She'd found her mother's favorite spot and she'd stood there, her eyes shut tight, trying to feel as if she belonged here. With her feet in the Kansas dirt and her face to the Midwest sky.

As if, finally, she'd found her home.

But the only thing she felt there inside of her was Joaquin. So intently, so completely, that she'd jumped slightly where she stood, convinced that she could feel his hands upon her—

Yet when she opened her eyes and turned clear around the circle, she was alone.

Even now, in a sleek car crawling through traffic into Central London, she could hear Catherine's voice in her head the way she had that day. *Love. Love is a gift. You must not squander it.*

Amalia had heard all the things that Joaquin had said to her on the island. She knew that he'd meant them. And she might like to think, in the privacy of her own hopes and dreams, that he could not possibly remain this darkly furious with her if he did not feel *something*...

But if she knew anything in this life, it was that one person could not change another. Her own upbringing at the hands of one of the most stubborn women alive had taught her that. And besides, she'd spent five years trying to change her own mind. Her own heart.

All she could do was accept the gift that had been given to her, or not.

Amalia only needed to make certain that no matter what she did, she honored it. That she did not squander it. That she did not walk away from it, simply because it didn't look the way she thought it should.

She had dressed like the royal princess she no longer was today, though she'd left her hair down because he liked it. She had the car drop her off at the sleek office building in the city, where she knew he kept his offices instead of at his home. Amalia suspected she was far more likely to be able to talk her way past a receptionist than any domestic staff who were, in her experience, far more keen about protecting their employers' privacy.

And when she was ushered into Joaquin's office to find him sitting there, his green eyes glittering while all of London lay at his feet through the windows behind him, Amalia smiled.

"I told you what would happen if you left," Joaquin growled at her.

Which, she couldn't help but notice, wasn't the same thing as summoning security, having her thrown out, or having refused to allow her entry into his office in the first place.

She took that as an encouraging sign.

"London is *an* island," she said. "But it's not *your* island. Not just yet."

"Amalia," he began, in that commanding way of his.

And she told herself that this was love, not addiction. That this was freedom, because she'd chosen it this time. Maybe, she could admit in retrospect, she'd secretly hoped that Joaquin would turn up on the island when she'd returned to it. This time, she'd sought him out directly. It wasn't happenstance. It wasn't luck or coincidence.

It was love, she told herself. And maybe that was the real freedom.

So she unwound her wrap from around her shoulders, then dropped it to the floor as she'd done before, secure in the tinted windows that kept his staff from seeing in. Then she knelt down, smiled at this man she was sure loved her back no matter what he might say to the contrary, and proved it.

CHAPTER NINE

HE HAD WON.

The facts spoke for themselves. It was incontrovertible. Amalia had returned. And it was not lost on him that she had marched straight into his offices, given her name, and made no attempt to conceal her identity when she'd sought him out. That pleased him more than he chose to let on.

He'd won, damn it, and he lived to win.

Though for some reason, now that Amalia was back with him—if in London rather than Cap Morat, a pity only because it meant she wore more clothes—Joaquin could not access that sense of victory he knew he deserved to feel.

"What did you do today?" he asked her one night.

It was late. He had found himself impatient in the midst of closing a major deal, which was unusual for him. Those were the moments he lived for, normally. But nothing was normal these days. Not when he had Amalia living with him in his bright, modern Southwark penthouse, three floors overlooking the Thames that he rarely thought of at all while he was traveling, and now could hardly bear to leave.

He'd found her in the library he kept on the second level tonight and had joined her there, pouring himself a generous measure of Izarra before sitting on one of the notably uncomfortable midcentury armchairs near the gas fire that was made to look like an art installation, not a fire. Another decorator's touch he hadn't cared about enough to decline.

Something he hadn't explained to Amalia when he'd first brought her here. She had looked around, clearly wondering how the same man who could fashion himself something cozy in half-submerged cells could also live here, in this flat of planes and angles and architectural flourishes designed to be looked at, not lived in. For a man who was always at the office, it was nice to come home to a place that was especially created to make it clear that whoever lived here had both wealth and other homes.

But he knew that if he explained all this

to Amalia, she would read things into it. He didn't want that.

Or he hadn't wanted that at first. Now he was less sure.

"I went shopping," she told him, looking offensively comfortable in the brutal chair she sat in. And she said it in tones of awe, as if she was confessing to taking up interstellar flight while he'd been pretending to pay attention in a contract negotiation. "It was the most astonishing thing. I simply…walked up and down Oxford Street. All on my own. I wore trainers like everybody else. No one recognized me. No even looked at me. I could have been anyone."

He swirled the liqueur around in his glass. "And this is a good thing?"

"I understand that you spent a considerable amount of time and effort becoming singular." Amalia's overtly blue gaze touched his. She did not touch the glass of Izarra he had set down on the angular table beside her. She glanced at it now, but didn't pick it up. She looked into the fire instead. "But I'm headed in the opposite direction. I was always singular. And now I must learn how to blend. And I managed it, all on my own."

"Then, of course, you have my congratulations."

Even he could hear how dark he sounded. How ill tempered. And he couldn't have explained himself even if she'd asked—but then, that was the trouble, wasn't it? She wouldn't ask. She did not push him.

He could not complain. She was generous with her body, her time, her enthusiasm. She had come back to him and she had been like a ray of light. A beacon through the British gloom. As if she'd gone off to America only to return with the Spanish sun at her disposal.

Joaquin had basked in her.

But weeks had passed since she'd turned up in his office. Having never entertained a woman in his home before, Joaquin should have paused before moving this one straight in, but he hadn't. He told himself it was because he wanted access to her at his convenience, that was all. Besides, he truly did wish to see if that all-consuming hunger for her that had left him feeling so unbalanced and off-kilter on Cap Morat would continue to affect him here, where it was usually necessary that he go into his office each day.

He'd wanted to see if he could handle it in the real world of London as opposed to the fantasy of Cap Morat. That was the truth of things.

At first Amalia gave herself to him the

way she always did. The way she always had. Fully, easily, generously. With that wildfire passion to match his own and that same near-desperation that never seemed to leave either one of them.

He had told her that the only thing between them was sex, and the sex continued to be blisteringly hot, magnificent in every way. That didn't seem to change no matter what country they were in.

It was when they were out of bed that he found himself… Not quite unnerved. That was too strong a word. But he felt on edge. Because at first she had been so bright, but lately, he had begun to notice that she seemed dimmer. Quieter.

Though when he asked, she always smiled wide and told him she was fine. Then usually loved on him some more.

Why wasn't he satisfied with that? Had he not dreamed of this?

"It is like this library of yours," she was saying now, in that perfectly pleasant way she said everything. But he didn't believe the *pleasantness*. Not when he had watched summer ease away, out of her blue eyes, as one week bled into the next. He felt as if he was losing her when she was *right here*. It was maddening. "You take such pleasure in waving your lack of pedigree and education as a flag. This library tells a different tale."

Joaquin hadn't expected that. His heart, that useless, traitorous organ, began to clatter in his chest.

"I am merely aping my betters," he said quietly. But not without an edge to his voice that he couldn't seem to dispel. "Is that not the fantasy of the upper classes? That, given the opportunity, all of us peasants would try our best to fit in with them? If we could, that is."

"I can't speak to the psychology, Joaquin."

He was certain he did not mistake that faintly chiding note in her voice. But no matter how he studied that beautiful face of hers, he could not seem to crack the code. Amalia was too serene. Too distant. She'd come back to him a ghost in every way but one.

His need for her never eased. But he wanted *her*. Not this version of her who gave him everything he'd said he wanted, but was not the Amalia he craved—raw and undone and always so luminous, in bed and out.

Not the Amalia he still—

But he cut that off. With prejudice. He'd loved her once, yes. But that had been a long time ago. He knew better now.

That edginess in him had teeth. He took another pull from his drink.

"Let me hasten to assure you that I have no desire to impress snobby blue bloods," he told her. Perhaps more harshly than necessary.

"You're the one who keeps talking of performing intellectual feats for others, as if they might be grading you," she said, still sounding *pleasant*. She looked as if she were simply having the sort of conversation anyone might over a cocktail. And she looked engaged, too—not that serene armor she had used so well on the island. Why did it all leave him feeling as if she was that edginess within him, teeth too sharp? "But there are too many volumes in this room with cracked spines and well-worn pages for me to believe that you have not spent a significant amount of time educating yourself. Knowing you, I imagine it gives you pleasure to let these upper-class blue bloods you so disdain imagine that they are speaking of things you cannot understand. When, in fact, you do."

"Snobby, upper-class blue bloods like yourself, you mean."

She smiled, and that should have pleased him, surely. But it only made the disquiet in him worse. The way it did more and more these days. "But I am no such thing. I am made of hardy peasant stock and can trace my lineage all the way back to the potato famine in County Galway. So I am afraid, Joaquin, that you will have to take out these class preoccupations of yours on someone else."

And she might have seemed more and more a ghost to him by the day. Because he felt as if she was slipping away even when she was right in front of him, though he could not point to anything she was doing to give him that impression. Just that the light she'd brought with her was fading—and how could he say such a preposterous thing?

He dealt in facts. Not feelings. Not *light*.

Still, there was one way he could reach her. He wasted no time standing from his uncomfortable chair, then going to pull her up out of hers.

"Shall I demonstrate these preoccupations, Princess?" he asked, his voice rough.

But she melted into him the way she always did.

And so he did his best to bring them both alive, right there on his library floor.

The days rolled by. He flew to Hong Kong. To New York. To Perth and back. And whether he took her with him or left her behind, it did not seem to matter. Nothing could make her glow again the way she had.

Not even him.

Telling himself that this was the sweetness of victory and he ought to enjoy it didn't help.

Nor did the notion he had, often, that she was *trying* to find her sparkle in there somewhere. Trying and failing.

One evening he wrapped up his meetings, then returned to the hotel he owned in Singapore. He found her in the private pool attached to the presidential suite, a sleek shape as she cut through the dark water, swimming laps with the skyline looking on.

Joaquin did not alert her to his presence. He stayed where he was, watching her move back and forth. And his heart ached inside him, making it entirely too clear to him that he was missing something. When he prided himself on never missing a thing.

Back and forth she went, slicing her way through the water, her black hair streaming out behind her like ink.

She stopped at one end and stayed there a moment, then two, her gaze out on the city. And when she turned around again, she started when she saw him standing there. But Joaquin found himself focusing on the puffiness of her eyes.

"Have you been crying?" he demanded.

The notion was unacceptable. It made the edginess in him scrape, hard.

"Why would you ask me that?" She lifted her fingers to her face and pressed, there above her cheekbones. "It must be the chlorine."

"Must it?"

Amalia looked at him for far too long, standing there in the water like some kind of selkie, his favorite myth. Yet this was not a moment for fantasy. Something about the blue of her gaze connected too hard to that ache inside him.

Like a blow.

For a moment Joaquin thought he might have swayed where he stood, but that was impossible. He did not *sway.*

She swam to the ladder nearest him, ducked her head back into the water, and smoothed back her hair. Then she rose and as she did, he realized that she was naked.

And he ceased noticing or caring if he swayed on his feet.

"What could I possibly have to cry about?" Amalia asked, her voice soft, but inarguably sultry.

And he thought, *She's using sex as a weapon.*

Just as he liked to do.

He wasn't sure he cared for it—but it was a weapon that worked.

On him as well as her.

And they had been back in London for some while when he remembered that night in Singapore again. The pool. Her eyes red from some emotion she chose not to share with him, when once she would have fought to keep her composure, only to tell him anyway. In one way or another.

Joaquin was astounded to find that he wanted her to tell him everything.

He had instituted nightly dinners and often found himself attempting to make conversation like he was…someone else. *Like you are as she was,* a voice in him liked to point out. *So desperate. So needy.*

But he refused to accept those things were true, so he dismissed them.

Tonight she had been waiting for him in the foyer when he'd come in from the office, dressed in what he knew she'd once considered her armor. All princess, no peasant.

Joaquin understood at once that she had decided to have a conversation with him. At last.

But he had no desire to talk, suddenly. Not if she felt she needed to wear armor to do it.

"I'm famished," he told her shortly.

And when she only smiled that damned smile at him, he'd stomped up the stairs, finding his way to the dining alcove he always preferred. Because it was a narrow stretch of bright wood on one side and glass on the other, and he could pretend that all of not-so-giddy London on the other side of that glass—from Blackfriars into the City—was just another ocean.

As indifferent, as inexhaustible.

But even a full belly could not make him feel easy about the way she looked at him, no hint of summer in her blue eyes.

"You clearly have something you wish to tell me," he bit out at the end of the meal, sitting back in his chair and trying not to look as if he was bracing himself. When he was. "That will make a change, I imagine, from all these weeks of silence."

Amalia frowned. "What silence do you mean? We speak all the time."

"Indeed we do. Of nothing consequential."

"Joaquin. You've made it very clear that intimacy of any kind is unacceptable to you. Or did I misunderstand?"

He could feel his jaw tighten. "You did not."

And, of course, she replied with that smile that went nowhere near her eyes. When once upon a time, it had transformed her whole face—and him, too.

But he knew of only one way to pry it from her lips, and she wanted to *talk* instead.

"I have excellent news," she told him, and he knew, instantly, that he would not agree with that description. "I have been in touch, cautiously, with Delaney Clark. The true Crown Princess, heiress to the Ile d'Montagne throne."

"I know who Delaney Clark is, Amalia."

She acknowledged that with the faintest inclination of her head, though gave no sign that she could hear his foul tone of voice. Which made him feel precisely how he did not wish to feel—like a grubby commoner who might ruin the fine lady's hem with his peasant fingers.

Not a feeling he had ever anticipated having in a flat last valued to the north of eight million quid. That he'd paid for in cash.

"I liked her during our single interaction back on the island," Amalia was telling him. "But it was hard to tell, really, what I felt about anything. That single interaction was a performance, and everything around it was… fraught. Anyway, after going to Kansas, it began to seem silly that she and I weren't some kind of resource to each other." Her lips twisted into something rueful. "She was the one who reached out, actually."

"That makes sense," Joaquin said, feeling his way to solid ground again. "It is far easier to step into the shoes of a farm girl than a princess."

She looked at him a moment or two too long. "Well. Precisely. I'm glad that was so obvious to her and to you, apparently. It had not occurred to me."

"Because you were the one who was demoted, Amalia." And he meant that kindly. Even his voice was softer, of its own accord. "Nobody has a roadmap for Cinderella stories in reverse."

And he could have sworn that Amalia looked…stricken, then. She swallowed, almost as if it hurt, and he waited while she took a sip from her wineglass.

Though he could admit that he was not saddened to see something—anything—on her face that was, if not the light he wanted, something different. Something that broke through her composure in the way he'd long thought only he could—and usually only in the bedroom.

"Delaney has offered me a position," she told him.

And of all the things he might have imagined Amalia wanted to say to him, none of them were that. "I beg your pardon?"

"She and Queen Esme wish to appoint me to a newly formed role. As a minister." And he watched, as if from a great distance, as she sat straighter in her chair. Squaring her shoulders the way she did when she was *working*. As if this conversation was a *job*. "Delaney needs someone who can prepare her for the role she must assume, but it must be someone she trusts. Someone without ambition, or the desire to sell her out to the tabloids. There is really only one person alive who fits the bill."

"Why should she trust you?" His voice dropped the temperature in the room by at least twenty degrees, which at least matched the chill within him then. "She is the reason you were cast out of the only home you have ever known."

"That is not exactly true." Amalia folded her hands in front of her. "Delaney is as much a victim of circumstance as I am. It was her husband who uncovered the truth about her parentage and mine. He is the one who went to Kansas to fetch her and put all of this into motion. She had nothing to do with it."

"Then you are either the most altruistic saint who has ever blessed this earth," he growled at her, "or a fool."

"Thank you," Amalia retorted, her voice

clipped and her eyes ablaze—but at least that was light. "I appreciate your support, Joaquin. In this and all things."

And everything inside of him…imploded.

All that fire. All of these bleak weeks that he should have enjoyed to the fullest. The way she had haunted him across five years, and haunted him still, though she was right front of him.

The way she'd cried in a pool in Singapore and denied it, right to his face.

And all the while there was that ache inside him that he could not vanquish, no matter how he tried.

If he could have, he would have roared loud enough to shatter all the glass in this penthouse of his. In all of London, come to that.

Instead, he focused on Amalia.

On the way she watched him, too shrewdly, as if she knew every single thought that crossed his mind. As if she could feel all those things inside of him herself.

As if she knew, damn her, and was doing this anyway.

"I take it that this is not a remote position," he managed to bite out. "If you wish to leave me yet again, Amalia, I wish you would come out and say it."

"How?" she asked him, and he had never heard her use that tone before. It seemed to knock him over, though he knew he was upright. He was winded, and it took him a long moment—and a roaring in his ears—to understand why. It was the softness in her voice. It was the starkness of her gaze. It was as if he had never seen her before, not like this. Unadorned. Without her armor. "How do you think I ought to reach you, Joaquin? When you do not wish to be reached?"

He wanted that to be a slap. A fight. But it wasn't.

She was genuinely asking him these questions. As if her life depended on it—but she wasn't desperate. Not the way he remembered being when his life had been on the line. Too many times.

Not Amalia. She was showing him her softness. Her hope. With no apparent care for her own safety here.

He had never seen anything so reckless.

Joaquin pushed back from the table and stood up, in a rush. As if he intended to do… something, but what was there to do? Flip his own table? Demand that she love him more than the palace that had expelled her when he had expressly forbidden it?

Order her to protect herself better? When he had just bemoaned her armor?

"You've been here for weeks," he threw at her instead. "*Weeks.* Do you really believe that is a privilege I grant to just anyone?"

"I know you don't," she replied, and he could see the torment in her gaze from across the table. He could feel inside his own chest, as if he was the one doing this to the both of them. "But then, this is my punishment, isn't it? This is what you wanted all along. To make me pay. To keep me close, as close to tethered to you as possible, while you give me nothing in return. So how should I reach you, Joaquin? Tell me what to do and I'll do it."

It would have been different if she'd thrown that at him in anger, clearly trying to hurt him. If she'd been fighting here. But she was only looking at him, her face vulnerable. Her gaze direct, and still too soft for his liking.

She was killing him.

"I have given you everything I know how to give," he hurled back at her.

And then felt as if she'd gut-punched him again, because that was a truth he had not so much as thought. Much less said out loud.

He had spent all these weeks focused on her. On watching her wither away before him.

When perhaps the real issue had been him all along, because what she wanted from him he couldn't give. He didn't have it in him. He had been forged by harsh, cruel implements and what she was asking for was a kind of softness that wasn't in him.

It had all been taken from him, long ago.

"It isn't in me," he told her, though his voice was thick. "These things you want, I do not have them."

He saw sheer misery wash over her then, though she didn't look away. If anything, she sat straighter. Her blue eyes glittered, and he wanted to tell himself those weren't tears—but he knew better.

She was *killing* him.

"Do you love me, Joaquin?" she asked him.

It was as if the world stopped.

He felt it jolt and shudder.

And then, in the wake of that, everything seemed to buckle, crack, fall apart.

He buckled. He cracked. He fell apart—and yet he still stood there with the Thames behind him, the blue in her gaze all he could see.

How dare she ask him such a thing?

"I already loved you once, Amalia," he managed to grit out. "It was more than enough."

Amalia stood, then. And held herself so still, so precisely, that she reminded him of nothing so much as a blade. Even though he understood, on some level, that it was not in her nature to cut him.

Perhaps that only made it worse.

"You only love me in retrospect, Joaquin," she said, and she was not yelling. She did not sound cold or distant. She spoke quietly. *Softly,* damn her, and he would have preferred violence. Shattering glass, broken crockery. Proof that he was not the only one so blackened and hollowed out inside. "Only to justify your fury that I dared live up to the responsibilities I had before I met you. Only when it served you did you love me. Only when you could use it as one more weapon against me."

He wanted to shout, but managed to keep from it. He would never know how. "You have no idea what you're talking about."

Not because she was wrong. But because the way he had loved her before seemed like a daydream to him now. Because what he felt for her was not a summer, so quickly gone. It was an ocean. Challenging. Deep.

Eternal, something in him whispered, but he couldn't allow himself to catch hold of that.

"But I do." She spread her hands out before her, but he did not mistake this for a surrender. "I keep coming back to you, don't I? I keep trying. I keep thinking I can love you enough that it won't matter how you feel in return. I keep telling myself that if I manage to love you in the right way, it will make you feel the same. It will show you the way. But it won't. All it does is hurt."

He could still feel the buckling. The cracking. The world falling out from beneath him where he stood, and all of that was better than the pain in his chest. The pain in *him*.

"Why don't you just say that you don't like the life of an anonymous peasant?" he fired back at her. "That all your adventures in blending in on Oxford Street make you feel normal. Interchangeable. And Amalia Montaigne, once the celebrated Crown Princess of Ile d'Montagne, cannot abide it."

She shook her head at him, her gaze too bright, now. It almost made him crave the dimness. "You're making my point for me."

"If you leave me again, it will be the last time," he warned her, because that was all he had left. "It will be the end, Amalia. No matter how many times you kneel."

And maybe it was just the world turning

again, that jolting feeling that rocked through him when all she did was gaze back at him.

So he could see the way her chest heaved, as if this was no easier on her.

That did not make him feel any better.

"If you have to threaten me to keep me," she said, very distinctly, as if she too could hear the noise in his head, "you don't love me. And I doubt you ever did."

He wanted to argue that. He wanted to shout down the building they stood in. But there was that starkness on her face and it was in him, too, and all he could do was stand there. Like he was made of stone.

Like he was that lonely fortress he had turned into a hotel, keeping watch on an island for invaders who never came.

And she was offering him a softness he could not abide. He would not. It was a weakness.

Surely how he felt right now proved that.

"Joaquin," she said, her voice thick now. And he could see that whatever haunted him, haunted her, too. "You don't love anything. And I fear if I stay, that emptiness will slowly chip away at me until I am as empty as you are."

And everything in him was a terrible din. An endless, brutal roar.

He wanted more than anything to fall to his knees for a change. To beg her to stay with him. To do whatever it took to keep her—

But that was not who he was. That was not the man who'd climbed his way out of literal gutters on the force of his will alone.

Joaquin Vargas dominated, he did not yield. Ask anyone.

"No one is making you stay here," he gritted out, though even his tongue felt bitter. "No one is forcing this emptiness upon you. By all means, Amalia. Leave if you want to leave. I will not stop you."

No matter how much he wanted to.

She let out the soft, rough noise of a small thing. Some kind of sob.

And Joaquin thought it likely ripped out what little heart remained in him.

But he didn't move. He didn't reach for her.

He certainly didn't *kneel*.

Amalia turned from him, her head high and her carriage sheer perfection, and began to walk away.

She stopped before she left the room and swayed a little herself, catching hold of the doorway with one hand. "Joaquin..."

As if, even now, she thought she could

make him crumble. And the horror was, he wanted to.

The noises inside him were not small, but he did not wish to let her hear them. She had already seen far too much of him. If she hadn't, this would not be so painful. If she hadn't, he could have avoided all of this.

"Are you leaving me or aren't you?" he demanded, because that was what he had always done. Offend, not defend.

It had made him a billionaire.

Amalia let out another sound, more ragged this time. It was unbearable.

But she didn't wait to see his reaction. She didn't look back again. She tilted up her chin like he'd tried to hit her there, and walked away from him.

And he told himself, again and again, that this was another win. Another victory. Another feather in his cap, whatever that meant.

The reality was that he sat back down in his abandoned chair and wasn't sure he planned to get up again.

Amalia did not return. He heard the security system beep when she let herself out, and that was the end of it.

He stayed where he was for a long, long time, until he felt just about as empty as she told him he was.

But at least he'd won.

There was that, if nothing else.

Joaquin sat there for some time, telling himself it was enough.

CHAPTER TEN

BEING BACK IN Ile d'Montagne felt like an out-of-body experience.

Especially when Amalia was picked up at the private airfield by the same palace driver who had always picked her up. But then, instead of taking her to one of the private entrances as she'd expected, he delivered her to the front of the palace where anyone could see her arrival. See it and report it to the world.

Someone was making a statement.

Amalia had to adjust her approach to, well, everything in a flash. Because she'd been expecting that they'd sneak her in the side door, cutting down on the possibility of any photographic evidence of her presence. Since she was likely still considered to be an embarrassment. *Our Fake Princess* the papers had called her.

The senior aides had never looked at her the same way again.

It had never occurred to Amalia that the palace might *not* hide her.

But as the car slowed in front of the public entrance, all her training came back to her in a rush. As if she'd never been away. How to exit the car. How to walk, with perfect posture and a slightly inclined head, to indicate respect for the institution of the monarchy as well as her own quiet confidence. She had dressed for the palace in an understated dress and unobtrusively elegant cashmere cardigan, even if her heels were a trifle too exuberant for a person who could make no claim to the throne. She knew the courtiers would whisper amongst themselves and say she had aspirations above herself.

But the good news was, she didn't have to care what courtiers thought about anything any longer. Besides, they would say such things about her no matter what she wore.

She was ushered into the palace's grand foyer and expected to be marched off to some reception room or other, where she would wait to be given instructions. No doubt by some or other member of the senior staff— and likely someone she already knew. She was prepared to pretend she felt no shred of awkwardness whatsoever, because, it turned out, the moment she set foot inside this palace she knew exactly how to play her role.

Any role.

Because she had always been very good at this.

She stopped walking when she realized no one was escorting her, and more, someone appeared to be waiting for her. And Amalia was shocked when she realized that the person standing there beneath a chandelier that had inspired no fewer than seven separate well-known poems was none other than Delaney Clark.

"Well, thank God you're here," the other woman said in her warm American accent, which shouldn't have surprised Amalia at all. And yet it did. When was the last time there had been Americans in the palace? Had there *ever* been Americans in the palace? Having so recently been in Kansas herself, Amalia found she loved it. "I'm making a mess of everything."

"You shouldn't even be greeting me," Amalia said, in tacit agreement. "That's the sort of thing you have your staff take care of, if possible. Just so everyone remembers their place."

Delaney was wearing a similar outfit to Amalia's. Amalia thought they both recognized that similarity in the same moment. And as Delaney walked—too briskly, too energetically—toward Amalia, it was impossible not to notice how similar they looked, no matter what they happened to be wearing. They both had long black hair. They both had blue eyes. There were differences, of course. The shape of a nose, a chin. Amalia was taller. Delaney had a spate of freckles across her nose.

But they could easily have been sisters.

"I'm an American," Delaney said as she drew close, smiling. "The only places I'm aware of are geographic."

"Welcome to Europe," Amalia murmured. "We like a hierarchy."

Delaney came to a stop before her, dropping her smile. Her gaze became more intense. "I know how kind you were to my mother. I won't ever forget that."

Amalia smiled. "If you mean the Queen, I've spent a lifetime being kind to her. If you mean Catherine, well. She's actually my mother, too."

"I can't pretend to understand how hard this must have been for you," Delaney said, her blue eyes no less intense. "For me, everyone keeps going on and on about my change in fortune as if every moment should be a nonstop delight. I'm a Cinderella for the ages, apparently."

That reminded her of something. Amalia made herself smile, though thinking of Joaquin hurt. But then, trying not to think about him hurt, too.

It all hurt.

"Someone told me that I'm Cinderella in reverse," she told this woman who looked like her and who was now living her life. "And there are no stories for that."

Delaney's gaze turned shrewd. And Amalia remembered the first time she'd met this woman, in a press call that had been all about flashbulbs and fixed smiles. Even then, she'd liked her. Now, though, she liked her even more—maybe because she'd spent some time in that farmhouse. She'd sat on that much-loved couch in the living room and heard stories about people Delaney had known and loved.

They'd exchanged lives more than once already. How could they do anything *but* like each other?

"It seems you came to exactly the right place," Delaney was saying. "Because it looks like we have a lot of new stories to write, you and me."

Instead of summoning the servants to escort her to a guest suite, Delaney walked with her. And Amalia was so involved in pretending not to be overwhelmed by being back in the palace that it took her a moment to realize that they were walking directly to her old rooms.

"You can't be serious," she said when they stopped outside her old door. "These are the Crown Princess's rooms." She remembered herself. "They're yours, Your Royal Highness."

"Call me Delaney, please." And Delaney shrugged when Amalia stared at her instead of proceeding into her old rooms. "I don't actually stay in the palace." At Amalia's look of astonishment, she sighed. "My husband prefers to stay under a separate roof than the one the Queen enjoys."

"I see."

And Amalia did see. Of course Cayetano Arcieri, sworn enemy of the Montaigne family for the entirety of his life—a grudge he had inherited from untold generations in his very blood—would not lay his head down in the palace. Not until it was his.

"Did you choose the dower house?" she asked. "I've always thought it would be the best place to live. Near enough to the palace, yet also far enough away."

"This is why you are the only person in the world I can turn to for help," Delaney said then, her expression fierce and serious. "You already know everything I've had to learn on the fly."

And this felt weird. There was no getting around that. It *was* weird.

But still, Amalia knew—just as she had in London when Delaney had extended this offer—that this was where she belonged. She thought of Catherine and the cornfields, and even though it was in complete defiance of all known protocol, she reached out her hand and put it on Delaney's arm.

"I was very, very good at being the Crown Princess," she said softly. "And it will be my honor to make you even better."

And that was precisely what she set out to do.

She spent her first few days sitting down with Delaney—because Esme was unavailable, she was told each time she tried to see her—and her seethingly ferocious husband, who looked at Amalia with frank suspicion. Which she returned in kind.

"This is not my idea," he told her, seeming far too large and dangerous for the elegant dower house.

"I think we all know it wasn't mine," Amalia replied, princess smile in place. "Or I would be the one wearing the tiara."

"It was my idea," Delaney told him, with a private sort of smile. "And it's a good one."

Cayetano and Amalia, born and raised to be mortal enemies, were just going to have to learn how to deal with each other.

Amalia set up an office in the palace. She knew precisely which staff members she needed to ask to join her, and which ones she would allow nowhere near this particular enterprise.

"I think this means you're my chief of staff," Delaney said one day, sitting slouched in the corner of Amalia's new office, wearing clothing that would likely give Queen Esme the vapors if she were to see it. A T-shirt reading MIDWEST IS BEST and a pair of jeans that Amalia's former aides would have removed from her wardrobe and burned, without asking.

"The Crown Princess does not have a chief of staff," Amalia told her. "That sounds like something a common politician might require. You are a member of a royal family stretching back into antiquity." She smiled. "I believe you can call me your lady-in-waiting."

Delaney sighed. "That seems a very silly name for all the things you do."

Amalia eyed the true heir to the kingdom over the span of her desk. "Here's the thing about real power. It doesn't matter what it's called. All that matters is if you can wield it."

"I take it the lessons have begun," Delaney said with a laugh.

And every moment she wasn't in the palace or in the dower house on the grounds with Delaney, Amalia was exploring. She'd decided that she did not wish to live in the palace, and certainly not in the very same rooms were she'd been a different person. She was a private citizen now. And she might serve the crown yet again, but that didn't mean she wasn't permitted her own life as well.

Besides, she had lived on this island her entire life, yet knew it very little. She knew what their main city looked like from the safety of her motorcade. She'd visited any number of sites and toured them, but always in staid and formal arranged engagements.

Now she had the freedom, at last, to walk anywhere she liked. To do anything she pleased.

At first she worried that the citizens would respond badly to her presence, but it was the opposite. Everywhere she went, she was recognized, but that wasn't a bad thing. People stopped to talk to her. Many complimented her for going away with such grace.

"I think I might've had a tantrum or two, me," said one woman she met in the open-air market.

"I would bring the palace down," vowed another.

"I might have lit a match," Amalia replied, smiling. "But I stamped it out again."

After she'd been back on the island for a solid ten days, she had narrowed down her favorite spots and toured the various neighborhoods—on foot, not in a royal procession. She bought herself a lovely little cottage on the hillside, where she could look at the palace but also the sea beyond.

And if she stood there in the first place she'd ever owned, just for her, and looked for the hint of an island fortress on the horizon... she couldn't really blame herself. That was the good thing about a heart so thoroughly broken. Amalia doubted that any more damage could be done to it. Why not stare at the horizon? Why not cry herself to sleep?

It was just life. Her life, like it or not.

"You must be some kind of saint," sneered her least favorite paparazzo one morning.

Amalia liked to walk to work, because it gave her time to clear out the cobwebs of the dreams she had each night, all of them featuring Joaquin. She got to breathe in the air that smelled as she recalled it, salt and flowers. She got to be a part of the island instead of in it, yet apart from it. And she liked to tell herself, as she walked along, that this was what being alive was all about.

Feet moving. Heart aching. Breathing in deep, and still, enjoying it all in its own way.

"I hope I'm not a saint," she replied, smiling when she really did not feel like smiling at all. "Doesn't that usually involve horrid death?"

"Want to tell me what kind of person gets kicked out of the royal family only to come back and set herself up as an advisor to the very person who kicked her out?" He shook his head, the odious man. "I'll tell you what kind of person. A snake or a con."

"Believe what you like, Maurizio," she replied, with an airiness she was delighted to discover she actually felt. Because as little as she liked this man, she really didn't care what he said about her. It reflected badly on absolutely no one. He could think whatever he wanted about her. "You will anyway, and I'm sure your paper will love that."

Later that day, after preparing Delaney for a series of engagements that were deemed ceremonial but would actually be a test, Amalia ducked into a salon she knew was little used to make some notes.

And when she glanced up again, the Queen was there.

For a moment she could only stare. Then she remembered herself, and rose to her feet so that she could execute a proper curtsy. And not the one she'd used to greet her mother the first time she saw her each day, but the kind of curtsy she had not been called upon to give before. Deep and low, as befitting a commoner before a queen.

"I think that by rights you are an American," Esme said coolly. "And as such are not required to curtsy to anyone."

Amalia rose. "But I still think of you as my mother," she replied simply. "And I don't have it in me not to honor you."

She'd meant that to come out lightly. She wasn't prepared for the fact that *lightly* wasn't how it seemed to land. It hung there between them instead.

Then, as she watched, Queen Esme of Ile d'Montagne, who eschewed weakness in all its forms…looked very much as if there were tears in her eyes.

"I hope you know," the Queen said after a

very long moment, and not in her usual ring-
ing tones. "That is, I hope you understand..."

There was a time when Amalia would have
leaped in to finish the sentence for her. To
save her mother from anything, even what
passed for her maternal duties. She didn't do
that today. She was a new person, wasn't she?

So she waited.

"I only know how to care about one thing,"
Esme said stiffly, still with eyes far too bright.
"This did not distress me overmuch, because
I raised you to care deeply about the same
thing. And I believed, for all these years, that
whatever I lacked as a mother I would make
up somehow as Queen. It never occurred to
me that I could lose you, Amalia. I find what
has happened..." She sighed. "It is unthinkable. I cannot fathom any part of it."

"Delaney will be a far better crown princess than I ever could be," Amalia said, and
she knew she would have said that anyway.
But she found she meant it as much when
Delaney wasn't in the room as when she was.
"And she's the rightful Princess besides. That
matters."

"But she has gone and married an Arcieri," Esme said bitterly. Then she blew out
a breath. "And she is not mine. Not the way
you are."

The old Amalia would have been replete at this. For a woman who was in no way demonstrative, Esme might as well have taken up skywriting with those two small sentences that set years of her life aglow in retrospect.

But Amalia was not the person who had stuck away from this palace, under cover of night. She was the Amalia who had knelt upon stone and walked through fire. She was the Amalia who had found a kind of peace in a Kansas cornfield and who had looked a stranger in the face and known her instantly.

She was the Amalia who had lost the man she loved three times. And had no hope that anything could ever change that. Some fortresses could be renovated and made into luxury hotels. She'd seen that with her own eyes.

But others were like the old fortress she'd toured right here on Ile d'Montagne two days ago. Once used by the coastal dwellers to ward off the mountain rebels, it had been impregnable in its day. And now was nothing but a ruin, worn away by sand and sea and beaten down by the sun. It was good for nothing but atmospheric photographs.

Amalia knew too well what kind of fortress housed Joaquin's heart.

She knew too well what she had lost.

And somehow, that gave her the courage to look Esme in the eye.

"That Delaney is not yours is a good thing," she told the Queen she would always consider her mother. "I was too much yours. I would have married one of those milksop men you chose for me and obeyed you in all things. And that would suit you well, I'm sure, but only as long as you live."

"It is my intention to live for some time," Esme said sharply. "Especially now."

"Long live you," Amalia said, with a smile. "But no one lives forever, Your Majesty. Even you. And how would our plans have left the country? A weak king and a new queen too used to taking orders? I think in time you will find that Delaney will be a far better queen than I ever could have been."

Esme sniffed. "Maybe she could have been, if it weren't for the warlord."

"You know that he is right to want to unite the kingdom," Amalia said softly. "And he might not answer to you, but then, he listens to only one person on this earth. Luckily, she is your daughter. She will do great things."

The Queen looked over her shoulder, frowned, then shooed away whoever waited in the hall with the tiny flick of one finger. Then she returned her attention to Amalia.

"You did not take such liberties with me when you lived here."

"I did not dare," Amalia agreed. "Yet another reason I would have been an uninspired queen."

"Then you do not miss it?" Esme's voice was sharper now. "Have you taken this role so that you can relive the glory that was once yours?"

Wasn't that what that toad of a paparazzo had suggested? He wouldn't be the first or the last, she knew.

"I will tell you a secret," Amalia said then. "Because you were my mother and you will always be my Queen." She waited for Esme to lean toward her, slightly. She did the same in reverse. Then she whispered, so no lurking courtiers could hear, "I don't miss being the Crown Princess at all. I much prefer telling Delaney exactly what she should do, and then retreating out of the spotlight into civilian life."

Esme took that in, a canny look in her blue eyes. Blue eyes that Amalia had always thought were like hers. But now, having spent so much time with Delaney, she could see that hers were an entirely different shade. More like the Balearic Sea, less like the calm waters of Ile d'Montagne's Royal Bay. She didn't know how to feel about that.

"And your sudden delight in civilian life and all its charms," the Queen said, as if she was musing. When Esme rarely mused. Commands were her preferred mode of address. "This would not have anything to do with your enthusiastic embrace of one, particular civilian, would it?"

Because, of course, Joaquin was everywhere she turned. Even in this conversation, where Amalia had not expected to find him.

"I suppose I should be horrified and outraged that you've had me watched," Amalia said after a moment. She shook her head. "But I find that instead I'm rather touched. That's as good as a love letter from you, Mother. Forgive me. I meant, *Your Majesty.*"

Esme did not exactly unbend. There was a considering gleam in her gaze. "You are the only one I intend to forgive for familiarity of address," she said, with a slight inclination of her head, as if bestowing a gift. "But Amalia. Joaquin Vargas? He is unmanageable at best."

"Entirely so," Amalia agreed. She did not say, *And that's why I'm in love with him.*

But then, perhaps she didn't have to say that out loud.

"You may have been raised to be a princess you are not," Esme said, and Amalia thought she sounded almost...careful. "But that still means that you have one of the finest educations in the land. You're poised and graceful. And you're in possession of a considerable fortune that will, of course, only grow over time. You could have anyone at all, child. Must it truly be an uncivilized Spaniard who has not one respectful bone in his entire body?"

Amalia blew out a breath at that. "I appreciate the warning," she managed to say. "But this is all a bit embarrassingly after the fact. The choice was not mine to make."

When Esme only gazed back at her without seeming to understand, she felt her cheeks turn pink, and not in the happy way they did when Joaquin was near. This time it was straight embarrassment. "He doesn't want me."

She was proud of herself for saying that the way she did. A statement of fact, not laced through with self-pity, or any kind of whine. Amalia was proud that her voice didn't crack and that she didn't split wide open and bawl. That she could state an unpleasant truth like that, and still save her tears for the privacy of her own cottage.

When she was not under the gimlet gaze

of a woman who would never approve of Joaquin in the first place—and would certainly not approve of any mourning for him now he was gone.

Esme seemed to study her for a long, long while.

So long that Amalia's cheeks lost some of their embarrassed pink.

The Queen appeared to come to a decision. She drew herself up. "This is not something I would have told you if things had gone as planned," Esme said. "I would have had it cleaned up, swept away. I would have made certain you never knew."

When Amalia only stared at her, Queen Esme waved a regal hand in the direction of the salon's casement windows. "I think you may have underestimated how much your uncivilized Spaniard wants you, after all."

And even though her heart kicked into gear then, pounding at her, Amalia felt as if she was trapped in some kind of iron grip that made it impossible to move. It slowed her down as she turned and headed toward those windows, making her feel as if she was fighting her way through some kind of quicksand. All she could hear was the drum of her own heart in her ears. She struggled to put one foot in front of the other when what she wanted was to run.

This particular salon was set up in the front of the palace, looking down over the ceremonial forecourt and beyond it, the grand square where the public could gather and often did.

But today, though the square was teeming with its usual number of tourists, stalls, and bored teenagers, there was a bit of a crowd at the gates.

Because a man was there.

And Amalia's heart stopped in her chest, because the man was Joaquin.

Her Joaquin, here in Ile d'Montagne.

Her Joaquin, except it couldn't be, because *this* Joaquin was on his knees.

CHAPTER ELEVEN

JOAQUIN VARGAS KNEELED to nothing and no one.

But this was about Amalia.

And when it came to Amalia, there were no rules. There was only having her or not having her, and he had tried both. He'd had her without giving all of himself, which had resulted in not having her at all, which was worse.

The one thing he knew was that when all the usual things stopped working, it was time for innovation.

Innovation or surrender.

And he had come up with a thousand crazy schemes to bring her back to him. He could kidnap her. It was frowned upon in polite circles, but what did he care about such things as *polite circles.* But he still nixed that idea, because he thought Amalia wouldn't like it.

He was a remarkably wealthy man. He

could hire his own army and storm the palace at Ile d'Montagne if it pleased him. But Amalia, again, was unlikely to support such an action.

Joaquin couldn't risk it.

Because she had left him in London and he had gone cold. Bitter. He had spent the first few days after her departure storming around his home and his office, verbally beheading anyone foolish enough to cross his path.

It had failed to make him feel the least bit better.

And at the strangest moments, he kept thinking of Amalia. Not in the usual ways that haunted his dreams, but in her two exquisite acts of surrender, both of which had completely disarmed him.

Both of them on her knees.

And both times, he had felt the same wonder as he gazed upon her.

Because he would have thought that kneeling down like that was an act so shameful, so subservient, that it should have made her tremble that she did it so gracefully. Beautifully, even. It should have made her seem less, somehow, in his eyes.

Except when she did it, it didn't seem like surrender.

More like its opposite.

Once that idea had taken hold, Joaquin hadn't been able to get it out of his mind. Like all his obsessions, save one, he knew that the only way to get rid of it was to immerse himself within it.

He hadn't known it was even possible to kneel down with no clear idea what might become of it. Even if he commanded them to bend, would his knees obey him?

He was Joaquin Vargas, who obeyed no one. He had built his entire identity on the fact that he alone walked alone. That he alone had always been alone.

That he was so powerful that the whole world ought to genuflect before him and often did, not the other way around.

But at some point, during another sleepless night in a cold and uncomfortable flat spanning three stories in a London that felt empty without one particular ex-princess, he faced the unpleasant, yet inescapable truth.

It was his pride that wanted power.

His heart simply wanted her.

Whatever it took. Whatever she needed.

Joaquin hadn't expected that he would argue his way into the palace. He hadn't been sure if they'd even let him into the country. But when they did, he delivered himself to that famous square out front that he'd seen on television too many times to count. Most of those times in the past five years, when he'd pretended not to be watching news reports from Ile d'Montagne, and yet had somehow caught every one.

Just for a glimpse of her.

He'd walked to the gates, ignored the guards, and knelt.

And he had convinced himself on the flight down from England that the moment he took to his knees he would feel better. He would feel whole. He would feel…whatever it was those smug holy people felt when they were finally living out their purpose.

He felt none of those things.

He absolutely hated every second of what could only be seen as groveling.

And Joaquin Vargas did not grovel.

But when the guards told him to move on, he was obliged to tell them that he refused.

"I am here for Amalia Montaigne," he told them, and let his voice ring out with authority and command. "I do not intend to move until I see her."

And there'd been no small part of him that was looking forward to the guards' reaction to that, hoping it would allow him to dust off some of his old street fighting skills. He could think of nothing he wanted more at that moment than to bash a few heads together.

But there were paparazzi around, which he'd anticipated. It was why he'd chosen this specific venue for his little display. It had taken them very little time to identify him, and the next thing he knew cameras were recording his every move—or lack of movement—and he was forced to stay right there, on his knees.

"Joaquin Vargas on his knees?" one of the paparazzi dared laugh at him.

"I take it you have not set eyes on Amalia," Joaquin replied, and the crowd laughed louder, with a smattering of applause thrown in.

And even as he said that he knew it would end up on front pages. Everywhere.

Some part of him welcomed that. Still, he was considering his options. Kidnap was looking better and better by the moment, especially when a few tourists ignored his death glare and took selfies right in front of him.

But then, finally, the grand front gates to the palace opened, right there before him.

And at last Amalia appeared.

Joaquin was vaguely aware she had not

come alone. There were people behind her, possibly royal people, but he didn't care about them.

Because she was walking toward him, and suddenly, he knew that he could kneel forever. And would, if that was what it took.

"Joaquin," Amalia said, in that way she always said his name. As if she was counting her blessings each time she found it on her tongue. "Since when do you kneel?"

"Is that what you want?" He was not surprised to find his voice rough. And so he opened up his arms, wide, hiding nothing from her or anyone. "Is that what it will take?"

He saw her look around, as if taking in the crowd. But when she returned her gaze to his, she wasn't wearing that perfect princess smile any longer. He could see all the emotion in her blue eyes, stamped there for all to see.

It was all right there on her face.

And everything she was, everything inside her, everything *Amalia* burned so brightly there that he wanted to leap up and hide her from these jackals. From the world. From himself, certainly. He wanted to protect her if she wouldn't protect herself—

And in case the fact he was on his knees

hadn't indicated to him what was happening here, that certainly did.

But he didn't have time to reel at that because she moved closer to him anyway, and then he took her hands in his. And then, as if they were all alone on Cap Morat once more, she dropped down to her knees before him.

"Now everyone will do it," Joaquin said, unable to be anything but sardonic when inside him, he could hardly keep track of that wildfire that surged through him. He wanted to call it lust. Need. Hunger.

But those were shallow words to describe what he felt.

They were also the least important part.

"I don't need you to humble yourself for me," Amalia whispered fiercely. "That's not who you are."

"I find nothing humbling in this," he told her, and was surprised to discover he meant that. "There is no weakness in surrender. You taught me that."

Amalia studied his face as if she'd never seen it before. "You know that I love you. But I love *you,* Joaquin. It's uncivilized. Unpredictable. Untamable. I don't need you to surrender anything. I don't want it."

"You shall have it all the same." He switched their hands, so that his were on the outside.

He tugged her closer, so he could get her face close to his. The way he liked it.

"Don't do this," Amalia whispered. "It isn't fair. If you knew how hard it was to leave you—"

"But you made it look so easy, *cariño*. Every time."

Her eyes flashed. "It broke my heart. More every time. I doubt there is anything left. And if you think that you can—"

"Amalia," he interrupted her. "*Cariño*. I love you."

Amalia's eyes, the color of the sea, went blank. Her perfect lips fell open.

"I love you," Joaquin said again, with all the ruthlessness and tenacity that made him who he was. He could hear the murmurs all around them, and *I love you* floating on the breeze as it was repeated and repeated. *Good,* he thought. Because this was different from long ago, when he had murmured endearments in bed and then shouted out his *I love you* in outrage during that parting scene. This was better. "I love only you. I will never love anything or anyone *but* you. Not because you left me and so it is the only thing I can use as a weapon. Not as if loving you sometime in the past and losing you anyway is any kind of virtue. I suspect it makes me a damned fool three times over."

"Never," she whispered.

But he couldn't stop now. He bent his head to hers. "You make me imagine that this world is fair. That the life I have led and the things I have survived are the price I must pay to deserve you. And I believe that. I do. I would willingly pay them all over again."

And this time, his name sounded like a sob. That soft, small noise he hadn't thought he'd get to hear again. He wanted to hoard them all.

"I will not be satisfied with a summer when you were twenty," he told her. "A few months five years later. Or not nearly enough weeks in a rainy London summer."

He lifted one hand to tug a tendril of her long black hair between his thumb and forefinger, then tucked the raw silk behind one ear. "I want them all. And I want all of you. No compartments. No rules. I want your body, but you know that. And Amalia, it isn't enough. I want your heart. I want your dreams. I want your hopes, your wishes, your mad ideas. I want to take your life and entwine it with my own, so that we are as close to one as two people can become."

"I want all of that," she whispered, and only then did he realize that her eyes had welled up with tears, and they were making tracks down her face. "You have no idea how much. But Joaquin, you don't want babies. And I want a family that no one can switch up on me. I want…" She took a deep breath. "I want everything, Joaquin. But you don't."

And a few months ago he would have agreed. Now he knew better.

He leaned his forehead against hers. "For you, my Amalia, I have learned how to be a man. You have taught me what it is to be human, and for that sin, I've broken your heart and blamed you for it. And still you kneel before me with tears in your eyes. Still you want me."

"In my whole life," she told him softly, so softly, when he knew he didn't deserve her softness, "I have wanted only you. The moment I was free of the palace, even if that wasn't what I had planned, I ran to you. I will always run to you."

"You will not have to," he vowed. "Because I will be right there beside you."

Her eyes overflowed again and this time he wiped away her tears.

"For you, I will become a husband," he

vowed to her, there on his knees in the full light of day. "And a father. And you know who I am, Amalia. The gutters of Bilbao could not contain me. I have never accepted a single boundary that was ever drawn for me. Anything and everything I dreamed, I made real. And there is only one woman on this earth that I would ever consider marrying. Only one woman who I, on some level, must want to bear my child. For I have never been so careless. I never will be again."

Amalia was crying openly now, but this was not the red eyes in the pool in Singapore. He knew she might feel many things, but she was not sad. She was not a ghost. She was right here, in his arms, where she belonged.

"This must be a dream," she whispered. "I've had this dream."

"If it is indeed a dream," came another voice, "I'm very surprised to discover that I'm in it."

Joaquin glanced to the side and saw another black-haired, blue-eyed woman before him, though she could not hold a candle to Amalia. No matter the dangerous-looking man at her side.

Next to them stood Queen Esme in all her glory, and he anticipated that she would look at him as if he was something stuck to her shoe. But instead, the Queen nodded her head, as if bestowing her blessing, and even smiled.

And when he looked back to Amalia, she looked as full of wonder as she ever had that first summer. She looked bright and wild, the way she should.

"Marry me," he demanded, because he could do nothing else. "Live with me, Amalia, and let us spend every moment we have together fully alive."

"Not merely existing," she whispered.

"Never," Joaquin promised. "Not as long as we draw breath."

And he waited there, on his knees before a palace, while the only princess he had ever loved gazed back at him.

He would wait forever.

And then, a smile breaking across her face, Amalia threw herself fully into his arms. Then she looped her arms around his neck, and kissed him.

As if, together, they'd written themselves a brand-new fairy tale. The one about a man like a wolf and the perfect princess who'd tamed him by not taming him at all, but loving him as he was, no matter how he snarled.

And then, together, they'd won.

Because there was only one way a story like that could ever be won.

With true love…and forever not far behind.

Joaquin couldn't wait.

CHAPTER TWELVE

QUEEN ESME INSISTED on throwing Amalia a wedding. She brought Catherine over from Kansas, and Amalia knew that both she and Delaney were equally taken aback and entertained by the way the two older women, each powerful in her own way, danced around each other—and yet seemed to like the dance.

"I guess we really are sisters, after a fashion," Amalia said after witnessing her two mothers laughing together, when she could not recall ever seeing the Queen laugh like that.

"Oh, this is definitely our family," Delaney agreed cheerfully. "There's no getting out of it now."

And so that was how Amalia Montaigne, no longer the Crown Princess of Ile d'Montagne, married the one true love of her life in the Royal Cathedral where she had been expected to marry a tedious bore at her mother's command.

This, she thought as she floated down the length of the church in a dress that had made both of her mothers teary, *is much better.*

Because it was Joaquin who waited for her at the head of the aisle, looking deliciously disreputable in his wedding clothes, his green eyes glinting all for her.

And when it was done, not one, but two mothers kissed her and hugged Joaquin, too.

Amalia supposed that all the papers the next day would try to outdo each other with their clever commentary—though the swords had been dulled by the world's delight in Joaquin's kneeling response to yet another vile paparazzo—but, in truth, she didn't care.

Because she and Joaquin returned once again to Cap Morat. Only this time, they stayed in the honeymoon suite there at the top of the fortress. And the sensual pull between them would always be a huge part of who they were, but this time, though they enjoyed each other as they always did, their hearts were unguarded. They were wide open.

And so they talked.

They took walks around the island together, hand in hand, and it was as if they'd talked like this forever. There was no subject too grand or too small. They told each other stories, they made each other laugh.

They got to know each other all over again, the way they had that first summer.

The way, Amalia thought, they always would.

And that was what they did.

They put love first, and when they did, love followed.

They left the island sometime later, but didn't discover that Amalia was pregnant until a month or so after that, when they were back on Ile d'Montagne. Joaquin, who liked her cottage but preferred more room to move around, had bought up the properties on both sides and was already meeting with architects to create the perfect home for them. One, he assured her, that would not be filled with refurbished jail cells or uncomfortable midcentury furniture. He could fly in and out of the island as easily as anywhere, and it was nothing to go back and forth to London as needed.

"You had better build a nursery," Amalia told him.

"I told you that I want children," he said, looking at her intently in a way that never failed to make her knees go weak. "Your children. I do not go back on promises, *mi cariño*."

"I never said you did. But we'll be needing that nursery," she told him. And slid her hands over her belly in case he'd missed her point. "In about eight months?"

She was somehow unsurprised when her husband reacted to this news by swinging her up into his arms, spinning her around, and then making sure she was well and truly pregnant by taking her right there on the cottage's small sofa.

Their son was born a month before Delaney gave birth to a black-haired, blue-eyed daughter, the new heir to the kingdom. She and Cayetano named the new Princess Catarina Amalia, in honor, Delaney said, of two of the finest women she had ever known.

In time, Amalia gave Joaquin three more sons, each one of them more delightfully disreputable than the last. And she was not the least bit surprised that her beloved, who had never wanted a child, was such a good father to his boys that it could still make her cry. And often did.

But it was not until the eldest Vargas boy, the extraordinarily stubborn and too-much-like-his-father Roderigo, married Princess

Catarina that Amalia and Delaney stopped calling themselves sisters *after a fashion.*

Because they all became family in truth.

"And if I had to do it all over again," Amalia told her first royal grandchild, in the nursery of the palace where she had played herself, as a child, "I would not change a thing."

When she looked up, she found Joaquin standing there, watching her as he always did.

With love in his heart and written all over his face.

They had spent their life *alive,* and had fought to keep from squandering love along the way. They had treated their life, their love, and their happiness as gifts.

Because that was the way that *happy ever after* came true.

Every single day.

* * * * *

Even he could hear how dark he sounded. How ill tempered. And he couldn't have explained himself even if she'd asked—but then, that was the trouble, wasn't it? She wouldn't ask. She did not push him.

He could not complain. She was generous with her body, her time, her enthusiasm. She had come back to him and she had been like a ray of light. A beacon through the British gloom. As if she'd gone off to America only to return with the Spanish sun at her disposal.

Joaquin had basked in her.

But weeks had passed since she'd turned up in his office. Having never entertained a woman in his home before, Joaquin should have paused before moving this one straight in, but he hadn't. He told himself it was because he wanted access to her at his convenience, that was all. Besides, he truly did wish to see if that all-consuming hunger for her that had left him feeling so unbalanced and off-kilter on Cap Morat would continue to affect him here, where it was usually necessary that he go into his office each day.

He'd wanted to see if he could handle it in the real world of London as opposed to the fantasy of Cap Morat. That was the truth of things.

At first Amalia gave herself to him the

to Amalia, she would read things into it. He didn't want that.

Or he hadn't wanted that at first. Now he was less sure.

"I went shopping," she told him, looking offensively comfortable in the brutal chair she sat in. And she said it in tones of awe, as if she was confessing to taking up interstellar flight while he'd been pretending to pay attention in a contract negotiation. "It was the most astonishing thing. I simply…walked up and down Oxford Street. All on my own. I wore trainers like everybody else. No one recognized me. No even looked at me. I could have been anyone."

He swirled the liqueur around in his glass. "And this is a good thing?"

"I understand that you spent a considerable amount of time and effort becoming singular." Amalia's overtly blue gaze touched his. She did not touch the glass of Izarra he had set down on the angular table beside her. She glanced at it now, but didn't pick it up. She looked into the fire instead. "But I'm headed in the opposite direction. I was always singular. And now I must learn how to blend. And I managed it, all on my own."

"Then, of course, you have my congratulations."